GEORGE
JOHNSON'S
WAR

GEORGE JOHNSON'S WAR

✳✳✳✳✳✳✳✳✳✳✳✳

MAUREEN GARVIE

AND

MARY BEATY

A GROUNDWOOD BOOK

DOUGLAS & McINTYRE

TORONTO VANCOUVER BERKELEY

Groundwood Books / Douglas & McIntyre
720 Bathurst Street, Suite 500
Toronto, Ontario M5S 2R4

Distributed in the USA by Publishers Group West
1700 Fourth Street
Berkeley, CA 94710

We acknowledge for their financial support of our publishing program
the Canada Council for the Arts, the Ontario Arts Council and the
Government of Canada through the Book Publishing Industry
Development Program (BPIDP)

ONTARIO ARTS COUNCIL
CONSEIL DES ARTS DE L'ONTARIO

National Library of Canada Cataloguing in Publication Data
Garvie, Maureen McCallum
George Johnson's war
Includes bibliographical references.
ISBN 0-88899-465-6 (bound).--ISBN 0-88899-468-0 (pbk.)
1. Johnson, George, 1768-ca. 1826--Juvenile fiction. 2. United
States--History--Revolution, 1775-1783--Juvenile fiction. 3.
Canada--History--1775-1783--Juvenile fiction.
I. Beaty, Mary II. Title.
PS8563.A6749G46 2002   jC813' .6   C2001-903208-0

Cover illustration by Greg Spalenka (www.spalenka.com)
Design by Michael Solomon
Printed and bound in Canada

To my parents, Martha and Don.

M G

To my father, another George, who first showed me
Fort Ticonderoga through the mist, and my mother,
Dorothy Jane, who always read "real books" to her
lucky seventh graders.

M B

CONTENTS

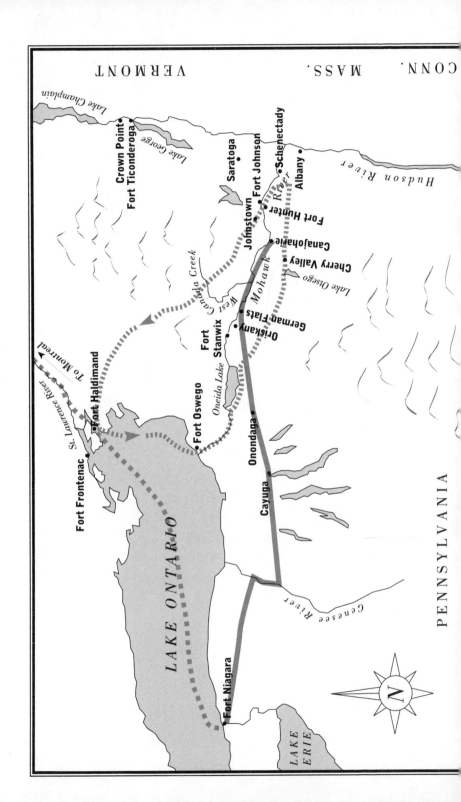

The Johnson Family's Journeys, 1777-81

The journey west, autumn 1777

George and Peggy to Montreal, 1778

George's raid, autumn 1781

Scale: 1 inch = approximately 44.5 miles
1 cm = approximately 28.3 km

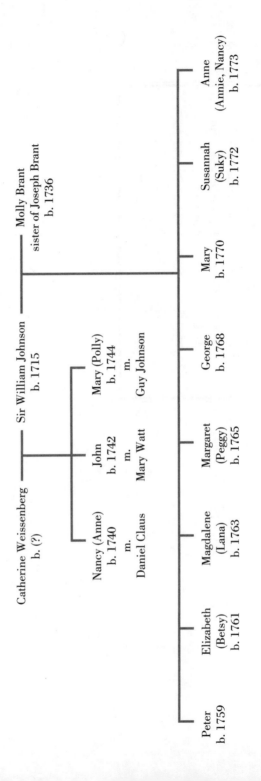

THE JOHNSON FAMILY

Catherine Weissenberg — Sir William Johnson — Molly Brant
b. (?)   b. 1715   sister of Joseph Brant
                                                    b. 1736

Nancy (Anne)   John   Mary (Polly)
b. 1740   b. 1742   b. 1744
m.   m.   m.
Daniel Claus   Mary Watt   Guy Johnson

Peter   Elizabeth   Magdalene   Margaret   George   Mary   Susannah   Anne
b. 1759   (Betsy)   (Lana)   (Peggy)   b. 1768   b. 1770 (Suky)   (Annie, Nancy)
           b. 1761   b. 1763   b. 1765   b. 1772   b. 1773

PART ONE
Johnstown, New York
August, 1773

IN *1773, more than two million immigrants from all over Europe lived in thirteen colonies along the Atlantic shore, on the edge of a continent populated by native peoples. The lands from the Mohawk River to the Finger Lakes were the home of the Iroquois or Haudenosaunee, united in a confederacy that included the Mohawk, Seneca, Oneida, Onondaga, Cayuga and Tuscarora nations. These tribes lived side by side with small numbers of French, Dutch, German and English settlers for hundreds of years.*

Though the Iroquois still hunted in their ancestral grounds, many had also become skilled farmers. Some wore European clothes and built frame houses in their palisaded villages. They sent their children to schools and often worshiped in mission churches. At the same time, most maintained their traditional clans and longhouse culture.

William Johnson became a great friend of the Iroquois after arriving from Ireland in 1738 to manage his uncle's estate on the Mohawk River. Handsome, friendly and adventurous, William soon learned native languages and customs and was adopted by the Mohawk as a brother. They sold him land, and as the French and British continued to struggle for control of North America, they joined him in fighting on the British side in the Seven Years' War (1756-63).

William became Superintendent of the Northern Department of Indian Affairs and the first baronet of New York. He fathered many children, including several with Mohawk women and three with Catherine Weissenberg, a young German immigrant. After her death he began another family with Molly Brant, stepdaughter of a Mohawk chief and sister of Joseph Brant. Molly helped William in his dealings with the Six Nations. William negotiated the Treaty of Fort Stanwix, which attempted to stop white settlement on territory belonging to the native people.

But many Americans who had helped oust the French were angry that they were now being taxed, in part to cover the costs of keeping them out of Indian lands. In 1770 resentment erupted. Citizens in Boston attacked the British soldiers and drove the tax collectors out of town.

Yet beyond Albany, on the northwestern frontier, the settlers of the Mohawk Valley were too busy clearing land and looking after growing families to worry about their hotheaded neighbors. And for the eight children of Molly Brant and Sir William Johnson, life in the family mansion was comfortable and carefree. Watched over by black servants, they amused themselves with pets, games and music as their father made plans for their education.

They did not know all this was about to change, as the War for American Independence loomed.

~ 1 ~
THE WILL

PETER and I rode down to the river while our sisters were still dreaming in bed. We set out from the Hall at a canter, the dogs snuffling alongside, birds singing away. I was pleased it was just the two of us, none of his friends or anyone else along. We took the back way to the river, stopping to pull up a bag of baby eels he'd left in the creek. I wiggled one out of the sack and threw it at him.

"Don't waste your bait!" he called back at me. "You'll have to catch your own eels when I'm off to Philadelphia."

That was how he told me he was leaving.

I pulled my pony up sharp and he skittered sideways, dancing in the air.

"Easy, easy, Pinch!"

Peter reached across and grabbed my reins and wheeled us round and round, till Pinch put his head down and began to chew the grass. My brother threw the reins back over.

"Why'd you pull up so?"

"You're going away again!" I was near wailing.

"Philadelphia's days and days away. You won't be home for weeks!"

"More 'n that. I won't be home till spring." He saw my face. "Georgie, I'm near fifteen. I got to make my way."

"But why d'you have to go so *far*?"

"Father's found me a good situation. I'm set to learn trade and business and such. Philadelphia's a grand place for all that."

"Who'll take me eeling?" The thought of his leaving grew bigger. "You said we'd go after ducks. You said you'd teach me to shoot." Then the worst thought. "I'll be here all winter long, with only *sisters*!"

"And a houseful of 'em, too!" he grinned, wheeling his horse about and calling out over his shoulder. "A lawn-full, a parlor-full, a *ballroom*-full of sisters!"

That made me laugh. I gave Pinch a kick and trotted after.

"Betsy will soon be turning heads," he said. "There's many'll line up to dance her up and down."

"But Lana dances like a crow. Her elbows stick out, and her head's all over one side like *this*." I flapped my arms.

"And Peggy *sounds* like a crow. Kkkaawk!" he croaked. "Kkkaaaawk! Kkkaawk! Dance with me! With meeeee!" He gave his horse her head and galloped down the hill, cackling and cawing, his pigtail flying in the morning sun. I caught up to him at the creek, and we made our way to the river.

At the bass pool we laid the gill net on the bank and trimmed a couple of saplings and threaded them through for stakes.

"You bait the net while I tie on the weights," Peter said. The baby eels squirmed like mad, but I got them all hooked and hardly any got away from me. When we were done, he rammed my stake into the bank, pulled off his boots and waded upstream, pulling the net out behind him.

"Hold up, Georgie. Now you got to scare out the fish. When I say so, you put the fright in them."

I ran along the bank, looking for things to throw. Peter called, "Cast away!" and I threw sticks and rocks into the deep part of the pool. I found a long pole and whacked at the water and gave a few whoops for good measure.

"Ho, look at that!" Peter pointed. "That's quick!" The bobs were dipping under the water. Something was bowing the net out into the current! "Haul in," he cried. We tried hand over hand but what was caught inside fought back hard. The dogs barked and bayed, tearing up and down the bank. The rope burned my hands.

Peter was breathing hard. "Must be a monster — it's pulling my arms from their sockets! I can't even get a good foothold. Look down in the water, Georgie. Can you see? What is it?"

I peered into the water, but it was too stirred up. Then, right under my nose something huge broke the surface. I got one quick look — at a gray-green giant with a thrashing tail.

"Pike!" Peter shouted. "A big one. Hold fast, and I'll try and haul him in." He lifted the net and waded toward the bank, winding the fish up inside. "Get ready, now. Don't let him tear loose. You'll have to hook him when I get close."

I didn't get a chance. I was scrambling for the gaff with

one hand when my stake pulled right out of the mud. I grabbed for it just as the monster fish made his run.

I hit the water with a splash and went under, holding tight. The fish thrashed from side to side, pulling me along. I couldn't see, I couldn't touch bottom. I could only hang on. My lungs were bursting. The fish pulled me forward, and then it doubled back — right into my arms!

I was bound not to let our fish get away. I grabbed it round the middle, net and all. It twisted and turned like the devil, dragging me to and fro till I couldn't tell which way was up.

Suddenly I was gulping air, sputtering and coughing. Peter hoisted me out of the water by my hair and yelled, "Hang fast, George! I'll land the both of you!"

The monster fish bucked and heaved in my arms but I held on as Peter towed us to shore. I kept my hold until we were well out of the water. We dragged the net up the bank, and Peter knocked the pike on the head till it was still.

We lay in the grass, water streaming from our clothes.

"Your hand's cut," said Peter.

I looked and saw that the spines of the fish had cut my fingers, and the palm of my hand was red with blood.

"Doesn't hurt."

"You're brave," he said. "But better get you home and dress it all the same." He pulled me to my feet. "George, you are a wonder of a boy. No one will believe you went right in after him!"

But it was true, and soon half the Valley knew about it. Near twenty pounds that fish weighed out. The cooks baked it whole, and I sat at the table when they served it. Father got Peter to tell the story over and over.

"Took both my boys to land it, gentlemen!" said Father. "Plunged to the bottom to bring you dinner. George has the scars of war to show for it." He reached over and held up my bandaged hand.

"Here's a health to His Majesty, King George." All round the table they lifted their glasses. "And another to the great pike that lost the fight and graced our table." They drank to the fish. "And here's a toast to another George, hero of the river, who held fast!" They drank to me!

Peter winked across, and I was so joyed at this most remarkable dinner and remarkable day that I forgot all about Philadelphia.

● ● ●

It was a grand summer the year Peter left. I was just six, so nobody paid me any mind. But Peter said I was getting old enough to follow along on my pony and carry his game bag when he went shooting. It was glorious being alone with my brother, out of sight of all our sisters.

We had so many of them. There were eight of us together: Peter, Betsy, Lana and Peg, then me, Mary, Susannah and Annie. A boy, three girls, a boy and three girls. Father said we made a pattern like a two-string wampum belt — purple beads for boys, green for girls.

He'd already got a white family — Nancy and Johnnie and Polly — but they were grown when he met our mother. And he'd got other Indian sons like Brant Johnson and William of Canajoharie, but they were grown up too. None of them lived in the Hall, only us.

People said the Mohawk Johnsons was all good-looking, but it was Mother was the true beauty. She thought she lost her glory when she had the pox, but the marks on her cheek were few and no account. Sometimes she dressed fine, for important folk. She'd hold the bedpost and let the servants lace her up, shouting when Juba and Jenny pulled her stays too tight. Then she put on her silk petticoats and the gowns Father brought from Paris, and her skirts squashed against the doorframe when she came in the room. Father whooped and swept her into the air.

"Let that fat Frau Schuyler see you now, Molly!"

"And how will she see me? She does not care to come to dinner at this house."

"Curse her then, the high-nosed creature." Father gave her a kiss and we laughed.

When she dressed so, she looked nothing like she did by day. Her lips were red, her cheeks pink. Her hair was puffed round her ears and twisted up with lace, and she wore jewels in her ears and pearls from London. The gentlemen bowed when she came in the room, and she'd turn aside smiling and tell Cato and Abram to bring in the roast.

If there were no ladies come to dinner, she left the gentlemen to their drink and games and came to us in the sleeping room in her gown and small black shoes. Sitting in the candlelight, her voice low, she'd tell us who was there and what news they had of horses to trade and houses building and goods coming up and down the river. She'd make up words in Mohawk to say what presents they'd brought Father — wonderful curiosities like bones from hairy elephants, or brass instruments from London, or other treasures from the world beyond.

Peter knew most about that other world. He'd been over the mountains to study at the Indian School in Connecticut and all the way to Montreal to learn French and fur trading. Then he went to Albany for fencing and Greek, and to "brush his nose in a bit of society," said Father. But he always wrote to us wherever he was. Father kept his letters and bound them in a book.

When a letter arrived from Philadelphia, Father came out of his office and read it to us all:

Honoured Sir

I expect I shall be very well acquainted with the business in 2 years. I am in great want of a watch, as I have to come to diner & go early to the Store I don't know what time to go without one. I can report that Mr. Wade has bought an Extreme good Violin for me.

I hope the gentlemen are well. Please give them my best respects.

I remain your most dutiful and affectionate son,
Peter Johnson.

"Here you are, Molly. My dutiful son's sent his mother a letter as well, folded inside mine in his usual manner," said Father. "He's asked me for a watch. See what he wants from you."

Betsy sat on the step and read it out.

Dearest Mother

Please send me some Indian curiosities, embroideries with porcupine quills, or a tomahawk, as ladies and gentlemen here are very eager to see them. I would also be glad if

*you would let me have some French and English books to read at leisure hours, and the prayers Uncle Joseph wrote. I fear I'll lose my Indian tongue if I don't practise it more....
My love to Betsy & all my affectionate friends at Johnson Hall.*

Mother waited and gave Betsy a long look.

"*And to my dearest Mother.* Of course it says that too, Mama." Betsy laughed.

Mother held out her hand for the letter. Though she could write English a little, she didn't read much. I leaned over her shoulder, looking at the markings on the page.

"Does it say my name?"

"Not this time, Georgie," Betsy said.

Mother held up the paper for me to see. "This is your brother's schooling." She ran her finger down the marks. "Peter's hand upon the paper, his voice behind it. You'll learn to do the same, when your turn comes."

My turn? I hadn't thought I'd be going away too, some day.

"When's Peter coming home?" I asked.

But Mother only called Lana to parcel up the things Peter wanted. I ran off to the stables and climbed on the horse cart. Some day, when I was big, Peter and I would drive out together. In a brand new gig, or a sprung carriage. I jigged a bit on the seatboard, practicing.

We'd have a matched pair of blacks or roans, like Father's. And Peter would let me drive them. We'd put on a fine show, Peter and I, going about our business together, up and down the streets of Philadelphia.

• • •

The summer of the great pike was the last time things were regular and normal, before our world turned upside down.

Peter left in the fall, and after that not even the weather was usual. Winter came on fast, before the ducks were even off the river. The quilts on our beds froze to the wall and the ink went solid in the inkwell. Then spring came so quick that by May you could fry an egg on a tin plate in the sun. It was too hot for lessons. I fished all day in the creek with my friends or played with the new pups or hunted rats in the barns. My little sisters made houses in the long grass by the pond. The older ones waited till evening to walk to Johnstown and visit about.

Things were different in the Hall too. Father was sick again. It was his old war wound playing up, said Mother, the musket ball he'd taken from the French. The year before, he was carried all the way to the hot springs at Saratoga for a cure. But it only helped a little. He couldn't even ride a horse, and he missed Johnnie's wedding entirely.

This time it was worse, because he didn't leave his room. All day long he lay on his bed, bad leg on a cushion, papers from the red dispatch boxes heaped on the bedcover. Dr. Dease went up some mornings to bleed him. Juba carried the basin out and poured the thick dark blood on the garden. She said it scared the vermin off the beans.

Peggy and me hovered about. Sometimes Father would catch sight of us and roar, "Come give an account of yourself!" Then we could run in and stand by his bed.

"Scouting about, Georgie? Give your report."

So I'd tell him what I heard people saying, in and about

the house and grounds. When Peg interrupted, he'd rough up her hair and say, "Irish red, stubborn bred," and laugh when she bridled. Then we could chat a bit until the gentlemen swept in with more papers and we had to run along.

Folk were in and out of the Hall from dawn to night — Indians, traders, secretaries and soldiers, all climbing the stairs, wanting his attention. Trader Croghan had to be carried up on a litter to spare his gout. He yelled so when the men bumped the doorway that Father yelled back at him, "Give up your whiskey high life, Croghan, or you'll be on your back, same as me!"

Sometimes our uncle Joseph Brant came down the river with tall Reverend Stuart. They would pray for Father's health, and then we must have more prayers, after dinner as well as before, in English and Mohawk both. Mother sat up late with Uncle Joseph, trading news and complaining about Mr. Croghan and all the rest who bothered Father and tired him out.

Father had charge of the Indian Department army, to keep peace between the settlers and the Nations. He must make sure the hot-head warriors did not stir up against the settlers, and that greedy settlers did not steal Indian land. So many soldiers were about that our house was like a garrison. Young officers in red coats stomped about in boots and lounged in the front hall, jumping up to take baskets from Betsy. On Saturdays the company from the blockhouse up the hill marched down to dinner. Cato and Abram carried Father out to the lawn so he could review them in their new uniforms. I marched around behind his chair with a stick for a musket.

Though Father went early to bed, the gentlemen and officers sat at the table till all hours, drinking claret from the good crystal. Their voices boomed and they filled the house with smoke from their pipes. In the mornings I stepped over them in the hall as they slept among the Indians in their blankets.

One day Mother had enough. "Sir William needs his rest," she said and turned all visitors away. After that the house was quiet, the blue parlor tidy and empty.

Peg complained, "Must all the handsome young men go along with all the ugly old ones?"

Mr. Chew, the lawyer, came and stayed long hours in Father's room.

"Juba says they're writing his will," said Peg. "Father's giving us presents for when he dies. He's saying who gets the bay mare, and the sleigh, and the birdcage, and the piano and his telescope. Even his pocket watch with the bells inside."

"But Papa's not dying!" I cried.

"Not now," she answered. "But he might."

At last they called us to hear the will read out. Juba scrubbed us hard and put us in clean clothes. I stood along the wall, Betsy on one side of me, Lana on the other.

Father's oldest son, Sir Johnnie, came, though his wife, Lady Mary, did not. She was having a baby at Fort Johnson down on the river. Father's other daughters Nancy and Polly came, and their husbands Dan Claus and Guy Johnson, all with solemn faces. Nancy and Dan's son Billy Claus was there, and Polly and Guy's little girls. But my brother Peter was not there, though he promised he'd come home from Philadelphia in the spring.

"Molly, come stand by me," Father said in a raspy voice. He sat in his chair, a shawl about his shoulders even though it was hot. "Cato, bring chairs for Miss Polly and Miss Nancy."

He coughed and Mother frowned, but he waved his hand. "No matter, it is nothing." He coughed again and caught his breath and looked at us.

"I shan't make a long show of it, but best you hear my arrangements. I am reminded by good Reverend Stuart that death comes to us all. I have therefore arranged settlements for each of you. I intend these to support you and your heirs – and all those who depend upon us for their living."

Johnnie stood in front with his hands behind his back. His thumbs rubbed together, level with my nose. I could see his nails were bitten to the nub.

"Let there be no dissension among you. And you see to it, John," he added, looking at him direct. Johnnie's thumbs stopped rubbing.

Father waved for Mr. Chew to start reading.

First came Johnnie, Sir John Johnson, proper. He was to have the Hall, and Fort Johnson, and land and houses all the way to Albany and Schenectady, and many horses. Then came Nancy and Dan, and Polly and Guy. They got houses and farms and horses too. Father closed his eyes, nodding at each name, keeping count.

Next came Mother. Father called her "*Mary Brant, my prudent and faithful Housekeeper.*" She was allowed all the things in her room to keep, and Father's clothes, and farms and houses and money. And cows — everyone was to have cows. I thought I'd rather have dogs, or monkeys. We only had one monkey left. The other one that bit people, it sickened and we buried it behind the cookhouse.

Mr. Chew read on. A farm for Peter, and a mill, like Johnnie.

Then my name! *"George Johnson, my natural son, and brother to those before."* I got a farm as well, *"Number Forty-four, called "New Philadelphia."* My own Philadelphia! And my sisters all got farms, even Annie, who was only a baby. William of Canajoharie got land and so did Brant Johnson.

Why did we need farms? We had Johnson Hall and Fort Johnson and so much land that we scarcely took a step on any that didn't belong to us.

Now Mr. Chew was reading about the Highland and German tenants who lived on Father's land.

"I do earnestly recommend to my son to show lenity to such of the tenants as are poor; an upright conduct with all mankind which will, on reflection, afford more satisfaction to a noble and generous mind than the greatest opulence."

Johnnie stood up straight at that, but his thumbs still went round and round.

It was a long time before Mr. Chew stopped. Father opened his eyes, and Johnnie took a jerky step and shook his hand. Polly and Nancy got up from their chairs and kissed him. So did Billy and my sisters and so did I. Father called for the babies and patted their heads and kissed them too.

"My mind is much eased," he said, but his head

drooped and his eyes were sunk and hollow. Mother swept us out, calling for the doctor and a sleeping draught.

Everyone went about with long faces, for it seemed Father would die soon. But Betsy and Lana said no. And they were right, for in a day or so he was much better, and I forgot all about wills.

ALL the time that Father was ill, the Mohawk elders and sachems came to tell their problems to Mother instead of him. Sometimes there was angry talk. When would Father call another council meeting? White land-grabbers were rushing over the lawful boundary line Father had set at Fort Stanwix. They were staking claims on Indian lands. The elders complained of raids and burnings, even murders of chiefs.

Would the Great King protect the Indian as he promised? Were the British no better than the French? The young warriors wanted to strike back at the treaty-breakers, the elders said. What could their great friend Sir William tell them?

Now Father was well enough to get dressed and listen, he set a meeting date for a grand council at Johnson Hall.

All through June as the heat scorched the meadows to straw, Mohawk and Oneida and Onondaga arrived. Then delegates from the farther tribes appeared: Cayuga,

Seneca, Tuscarora. Every day runners came with belts of wampum and word that more were on their way. The important people slept in the Hall, and skin tents sprang up in the fields. Every morning from the sleeping-room window I saw more plumes of smoke rising from the cooking fires and counted more horses tethered under the trees. No matter how early it was, Father was already there, leaning on his stick and talking with the elders.

Granny Margaret and our Mohawk relations came downriver from Canajoharie village to help with the feeding. We ran about with our Indian cousins while Betsy and Lana helped Mother ready the gifts. The office was filled up with brass kettles, silver crosses, scissors, iron nails, combs, pipes and tobacco, knives of every kind. Peg liked the silver trade brooches best, all curious shapes. My favorites were the little clasp knives.

Granny Margaret came in to see the gifts.

"My daughter has a hand like a sieve," she said, nodding and running a piece of gold lace through her fingers. "It is a fine thing to be rich, and generous too."

Mother gave many presents, it's true, but she always knew who got them. She and Betsy kept close accounts.

●●●

The first day of the conference I sat at the edge by my half-brothers, Brant Johnson and William of Canajoharie. Johnnie, Dan and Guy sat with Father. The governor and the gentlemen from Albany lined up on a row of chairs under the trees, sweat dripping from under their wigs. Dan stood up to change Indian words to English, and sometimes Uncle Joseph took a turn, for he knew the tongues of all the

Nations, and his English wasn't mixed with German like Dan's.

Father could understand the languages too. His Mohawk name was Warraghiyagey, "Man Who Does Great Things." Back when he was well, he liked to put on Indian clothes and smoke and drum at the campfires. Today he dressed in his red coat and spoke proper English with the gentlemen, or the Dutch tonuge, or German, or whatever use was needed.

The first to give an address was the Seneca chief Senhouane. He had a sharp nose like a knife, and his face was rough-skinned from pox.

"Brothers!" he called out, and everyone quieted and listened.

"The Great King's enemies are many and they grow fast in numbers. They were formerly like young panthers. They could neither bite nor scratch. We could play with them safely. But now they have great, sharp claws. They drive us out of our country."

The whites were very wrong to break treaty after treaty, Senhouane said. He was grieved that they did so and that his white brothers would act so badly. "Brothers, if they must settle so near the lands of the Six Nations, the Great King must make them behave." Everyone agreed the King must do so. I nodded my head along with the rest.

The sun began to burn my ears, and I crawled away to where the servants were readying the food. Abram and Cato were turning sides of sheep and pigs and deer over the fire. Cato cut me some crackling and set me to drive away the dogs trying to snatch the meat. I begged to take a turn at the spit too, but I had hardly started when he raised his hand and yelled.

"Not that way, Master Georgie! You're turning it the wrong way!" I stopped my turning in confusion.

"You're unroasting those beasts I've been roastin' all morning!" he cried. Fast as I could, I turned the spit back the other direction.

"He, he, he!" I looked around to see Cato splitting his sides. It was a good joke on me, so I laughed too.

After the feasting the council moved into the shade. Now was the turn of a Cayuga chief named Corn Husker. He was even angrier than Senhouane, and the cause was the white traders' rum.

"My brothers, this drink makes our warriors into women, into children." Corn Husker shook his fist. "My brothers, our white brothers steal our senses and then take our lands. And then they say they have forgotten their words. They say they were words spoken from rum, not true promises sealed in conference. They betray us and have no shame. No more should these cruel, greedy men be allowed in the land of the Cayuga!"

All the tribes murmured and nodded and so did Father. The gentlemen from Albany shifted on their chairs and looked sour. A man beside me said it was because they made their money on rum and land and didn't want to give up either.

At last it was time for the belts of wampum to be laid down — long white ones with blue tassels and little ones made of purple shells. More pipes were lit to show the speeches were done for the day. Father came by me, leaning on his stick, so I knew his leg was sore.

"This is temperate and reasonable," he said to Guy. "I feared much worse. Help me to the house. I'm stiff from long sitting." The other gentlemen and the chiefs followed them inside.

All night long we heard singing and drumming and dancing. Next morning it was Father's turn to speak. He put on his best scarlet coat with the gold lace, and Cato powdered his wig till the floor looked like snow.

Father called for Mother to tie his silver gorget around his neck. "John has sent word Mary's time has come," he said, lifting his chin. "He will stay till the babe is born."

"He should be here when you speak," Mother frowned.

Father waved his hand. "No matter. He knows well enough what's in my mind."

By the time it was Father's turn to talk, the sun was fierce overhead and most of the shade was gone. I sat in the shadow of an old sachem who stayed stiff and upright, though sweat ran down his chest in streams. He smoked, which kept the flies off me.

Father mopped his brow with his handkerchief. He leaned on his stick and swayed. But when he held out his arm for silence, his voice thundered out strong and clear.

"My brothers! I speak the words of our father, the King. He wishes me to tell you that the outrages against you are the acts of a few evil men and not the wish of His Majesty."

Then he coughed. He could not stop and all leaned forward, holding their breath until he caught his own again. His face was as red as his coat.

He spat in his handkerchief and went on. "The King's agents will act at once to hunt down and punish those who are guilty of these evil acts against you, my brothers. This I promise." Everyone listened with close attention and nodded as the sun burned across the sky. Sometimes he stopped to cough again, but then he spoke on. It was a long time before he laid down belts of wampum.

As the pipes were lit and passed from hand to hand, Guy, Dan and Joseph hurried to him. Father steadied himself with his stick.

"Brothers," he called out hoarsely, "I have done. I will retire while the chiefs prepare their reply."

His red face was purple now. Suddenly it went gray, as if the blood drained out of it. He lurched and stumbled. Guy caught him, but people saw and ran forward. They watched as Father straightened slowly and without another word went up the steps on Guy's arm. Dan took his other side.

Just at that moment Mother came around the corner of the house. She was in her Indian clothes, her red tunic sewn with quills and silver crosses. She stopped telling the women and servants where to set the food, and I saw her look toward the door of the Hall. Guy had come out again and was hurrying down the steps, calling for our brother William of Canajoharie. He said some words and William set out for the stables at a run.

Mother pushed through the crowd. "What has happened?" she asked Guy.

"I've sent for John. William is the strongest rider."

With a cry she rushed to the house.

The crowd that had seen Father stumble watched William gallop down the lane. Senhouane stepped into Guy's path.

"Our brother Warraghiyagey is ill?"

Guy shrugged. "It is his usual trouble."

In the house the door to Father's room was shut. Low voices came from behind it. I crouched beneath a table, but one of the gentlemen saw me and shooed me out. Then I was stuck by myself in the yard, all my sisters in the house. I was afraid, and after a while I was crying. But no one cared, for everyone around me was crying too.

A long time passed before I heard hoofbeats. There was Johnnie, thundering up the avenue on a lathered horse, whipping as hard as he could go. He leapt off and the crowd made way for him as he rushed up the steps, his flying coat-tails all mud. I ran after.

In four steps he was down the hall. He flung wide Father's door. I saw Mother holding Father in her arms.

She looked up. "He's going, John." Then the door shut and the same gentleman caught me by the ear and flung me out again.

I pushed through the crowd to get round to the kitchen door, hammering on it until Cato let me in. He didn't pay me any mind but went on talking with Juba in a low voice.

"Still a mile to go and Sir Johnnie's fine racehorse went down all a-lather. It give up the ghost, and Johnnie had to run on his own two legs to the next farm to get another."

Then he stopped, his mouth agape. I heard what he heard. A long, thin, high note filled the air and rose the hair on my head.

Juba shrieked, "Oh, Lord, he's gone." The other servants' faces went stiff with fear. The wail rose higher, louder. The tribes outside picked up the cry. On and on it went,

all evening and all night, mingling in the darkness with the
devil shrieks of the peacocks.

I went to bed without supper, for no one thought to give
us any. In the hot room I buried my head in the quilt. Peggy
hummed and sang and moaned to cover the noise, but I
heard it still.

●●●

In the morning when I waked, the house was quiet. The sky
was blue above. Why was it so hushed? Why was I in bed
full dressed?

I remembered. I set my feet on the floor and went to
Mother's room. She wasn't there, only Betsy and Lana folding blankets and weeping in the pillows. John and Polly
and Nancy were in the blue parlor, but Mother wasn't there
either.

Peggy came out of the shadows. The door of Father's
room was shut again.

"She's with Papa," she whispered. "Granny Margaret
and the aunts are too." I put my ear to the door and heard
sobbing.

There was a tramp of boots and Guy and Dan came
down the hall. I fell back as they knocked at Father's door
and went in. Guy said to Mother, "Molly, the funeral must
go ahead."

Mother's voice was flat. "We must wait for Peter."

"We cannot wait, Molly," Dan said, more gentle but
firm. "So many are waiting in this heat. So many to feed."

On the grass outside, the tribes sat without speaking.
Mother said nothing, but in the afternoon she came out
of the room. Her hair was hanging and her face was

blackened. Her red tunic was torn at the shoulder, as if a knife had cut it. She went like that to the office and sat with Dan and Mr. Chew. She gave orders for the killing of cattle and sheep, the baking, the gifts, beer and rum from Mr. Tice's tavern.

"Mourning for the family should be sent up at once. The sachems and the chiefs are to have it too. William has it so in his will. Black blankets, armbands and gloves from the storehouses."

She sent for cloths and for a tub of water, and she and Granny Margaret went back into Father's room.

"They're washing him," Peggy said. And I bolted from the house and down through the gardens and the fields, and ran without stopping to the stream. I tore off my dusty clothes and splashed through the reeds, and sat up to my neck in the clear current.

●●●

Next morning a crowd gathered in front of the house and down the road — all the tribes, all the people from the town and country, wailing and sobbing. Jenny and Juba dressed us in stiff black stuff, hot and scratchy and sharp with brass pins. Betsy and Lana were still sewing on buttons while I waited in the front room, watching what was going on outside.

"Sit down, Master Georgie," Juba scolded. I did, but I could still see through the open window.

The grooms led Father's horses with the gun carriage to the door. Drummers in red coats began a slow drumming and the Highlanders blew into their bagpipes, making a terrible noise. People stood with their heads bowed in the blazing sun. Eight gentlemen, Governor Franklin in their middle, carried the coffin down the hall and out the door. Their faces were dripping and some of them staggered on the steps.

"It's heavy 'cause it's lined with lead so Papa don't swell up and burst in the church," Peggy said. Betsy frowned and shushed her.

Some Highlanders pushed forward, big as giants, and helped heave the casket to the carriage. The horses stamped, their tails switching flies. The women under the trees raised the wailing lament again.

"Fetch the children," someone called, and Juba pushed us to the door. The piper was leading off, followed by John, walking by himself, with his hands behind him. Then came Polly and Nancy, black cloth over their hair, and Colonel Guy and Dan and Billy Claus, wearing black arm ribbons. The governor walked after, with his silver stick.

We were next, Mother and Joseph and Granny first. Betsy walked by Mother and then came the rest of us. Lana held my hand, her bony fingers cold even in the heat. Jenny carried Annie, and that was all our family but Peter.

Mother's other relatives walked behind, and then came the elders, their faces painted black. More gentlemen from Albany followed, and Farmer Herkimer and Mr. Tice and Old Yost and the other sheriffs and judges. Last came the soldiers, and the townsfolk and the servants. Hundreds there were, marching down the lane to Johnstown.

The church was crammed and fiery as an oven. I squashed in our pew, Peggy one side of me, Mary on the other, so tight I could hardly breathe. John sat alone in

Father's place, looking straight ahead. The church door was open, the crowds gathered tight against it.

Fat blue flies swarmed in the windows and lit on my face. The air felt used up, and all around me folk were sobbing and slumping in their seats. Reverend Stuart made his voice loud to be heard. Father had gone to a better place where the rest of us would go soon enough, he said.

Now some were keeling over, pitching to the floor. Old Yost behind slipped and banged his head on our bench. I whimpered with terror, sure we were all going to that place along with Father.

Peggy felt me shaking. She gave me a sharp pinch and hissed behind her black-bordered hanky, "They're only fainting, George, not dying."

Finally it was over, and people left much faster than they came, in a hurry to get out into the air.

As we dragged back up the hill from church, a great purple cloud hung over Johnson Hall. The sky turned yellow and the wind flung dust and straw in our faces.

Folk crowded under canvas, drinking beer and rum. After a while Juba sent us to bed. Now it was almost as dark as night, and lightning flashed in the sky. Peg and I watched from the sleeping-room window. I saw Uncle Joseph under the oaks, sending out runners to the western tribes to tell them Father was dead.

Coaches carried away the men from Albany ahead of the storm. The grooms handed folk into carriages and helped them on their horses, and the hoof-beats and turning wheels mixed with thunder. An earsplitting crack lit our room, and a gust of wind flung cool drops on my face.

Then the sky opened and down came the rain.

Juba rushed in.

"Don't you children have no sense?" she cried, and lowered the window with a crash. She scrubbed at my face with her apron and bundled us into bed. But soon as she'd gone, I crept back to the window and so did Peg. At every thunderclap the horses whinnied and the dogs barked and barked. The trees washed back and forth like weeds, and people struggled to hold down the tents.

I felt a soft shape slip in by me. It was Mary, her eyes wide and fearful. She flinched as another lightning crack forked across the sky.

"Is Papa angry at us for burying him?" she whispered.

"'Course not," Peggy said. "We had to, on account of the heat. Papa's gone to heaven."

The rain fell harder. The sky was crying for Father, I thought.

NEXT day we stood for the condolence ceremony in the awful mourning clothes. They stank of boiled tar in the sun and the black stained my wrists like bruises. The speeches were long but at least it was not so hot, now the storm had come and gone. Then the tribes began taking down their tents and loading up their horses. They put out their cooking fires and headed to the river and the westward trails. By next morning all that was left in the fields was ashes and trampled grass and mud.

The house felt strange and empty, though gentlemen still came and went, talking and talking. Mother kept to her room and Juba and Jenny did their work in silence, wiping their eyes on their aprons. Betsy and Lana sat in the white parlor, pale and sad, and wrote letters. I waited every day for Peter to come home.

Juba said I mustn't go out and mess my mourning clothes. The girls weren't allowed to go to Johnstown to call on their friends. The time passed so slow.

One hot afternoon, as fat flies circled the rooms and

buzzed against the windows, I saw Peggy slip into the blue parlor. I looked in the door, and she was standing before the cupboard with the fancy glasses. She reached up and lifted one out. She held it to the light and twirled it so it threw rainbows on the Turkey carpet.

"We're not to touch those, Peg."

She whirled and screamed. "Don't be such a ghost, Georgie! Always creeping about! You almost made me break this. I was only remembering Papa with the fine gentleman and ladies at dinner." She held the glass to her lips and pretended to drink.

"Will they all be Johnnie's now?"

Peggy frowned in amazement. "No! They're ours."

"Juba says Johnnie's baronet now Father's dead and he'll move here to Johnson Hall and we'll go away. Juba says Lady Mary won't want the pack of us in the Hall and we'll go to Canajoharie to live with Granny."

Peggy clutched the glass to her heart, stricken. "No! It's not true! Live with Granny in her little house? How could we bear it, eating Indian food. *Tedious* food! Only corn, and corn, and more corn — and if we're very lucky, corn with a bit of meat!"

I didn't mind if we went to Canajoharie. No one would make me wear stiff black clothes there. Peter would come and we'd hunt.

"I could shoot squirrels for stew."

Peg made a horrible face. "It won't be nice at *all*! Granny's house is so far away no one will visit. And what will happen to all our things? It's so small we'll never fit." She glared and set the glass back on its shelf, but not far enough. It wobbled and tipped and fell to the floor, smashing to bits.

We stared in horror at the glittering pieces spinning on the painted blue floor. Had anyone heard? But no footsteps came pounding down the hallway. I picked up the pieces and tried to fit them together, in vain.

"Throw them in the woods. And don't tell," Peg whispered, fierce. "Promise you won't tell, when they come to count them out."

She moved the other glasses about on the shelf so it looked like none was missing. I put the broken bits in my waistcoat and climbed through the back fence to a secret place. It was a fallen-down tree with roots sticking in the air and the earth ripped up into a little cave. I pushed the pieces far under so no one would ever find them.

When I got back to the house I heard Peggy's voice arguing right down the hall.

"What about our friends? I don't *want* to go and live with Granny! I want to stay here."

"It isn't for us to say, Peggy," said Lana. She'd been reading lessons to Mary and Susannah, and she put aside the book. Her face was pale and pinched up.

"I shan't go to Granny's. *I shan't.*" Peggy stamped her foot. Mary and Susannah began to cry.

"Peg could go to her farm," I said.

Lana blinked at me, puzzled. "What farm?"

"Peg's own farm, that Papa gave her in his will."

"Oh, George," said Lana in a tired voice, "she can't live on it now. Those are for when we're grown up. At any rate we've got to leave the Hall, so I suppose Mama will take us to Canajoharie."

•••

Twelve days after Father was buried, Peter came galloping up the drive. His horse was lathered like he'd ridden it all the way from Philadelphia. I heard Betsy call out his name and we ran for the stables. I ran fastest, but stopped a pace short.

He looked different — taller. Betsy rushed past me and threw her arms round his neck. Lana and Peggy flew to hug him too. I clutched his coat-tail, the only part I could reach.

"It hit me so sudden," Peter said, wiping his eyes and freeing himself from our arms. "Everything just the same, but Father gone."

"Gone to heaven," Betsy said like Reverend Stuart.

"You've lost flesh, Betsy," said Peter, looking in her face. "How is Mother faring?"

"She's so grieved, Peter, it's awful." Betsy started weeping. "She's stayed in her room since the funeral, waiting for you."

He went straight up to Mother's room. I ran behind and saw him holding her, rocking her in his arms.

Things would be better now. Ever since the funeral, the house had been full of gentlemen talking of rents and wills and muttering about troubles. With Father gone and Mother shut in her room, no one seemed to see us. But now Peter was home, and he was not so easily made invisible.

Johnnie rode up from Fort Johnson the next day. He'd left off his stiff black funeral coat and was back in his farmer's shirt and breeches, just a black cloth at his neck.

"I wish to offer you and the children accommodation at Fort Johnson for as long you need, Molly," John said.

"When I've moved my wife and son and our effects to the Hall, there'll be room for you there."

Mother had a black shawl over her head though it was a warm day. She was sad-faced and her voice was low. "I have made plans to go on to Canajoharie. I will return to my mother and my people. I have my own lands there, and those your father left me."

John looked vexed. "There are necessities to undertake with Father's will," he argued. "The properties must be secured and your tenants settled. It would be better if you were not so far away."

"I place such affairs in your hands, Sir John," she said.

John dropped his voice, talking about strange goings-on in faraway cities. "There's worrisome things afoot, Molly. The news from Boston and Albany grows stranger every day. I cannot guarantee your safety away from the Department troops here. The rebels are getting bolder. Guy says they've started meeting in the town. We're being watched, all of us. It's not the French on the prowl this time but the rabble who follow Sam Adams," John went on. "The ones who dumped the tea in Boston harbor."

Mother shrugged. "Such squabbles do not concern me. How could I be safer than among my people?" She turned in her chair and her face brightened. "Son?"

Peter had stepped in from the hallway, come from the stable where he'd taken John's horse. He went to stand beside her, serious.

"I could not help overhearing. May I speak?"

John and Mother nodded.

"I must stay near to Guy with the position he has spoke

for me. Canajoharie would be less convenient for me to lodge. Fort Johnson's far nearer."

Peter was not going back to Philadelphia. Now that Guy was Indian Department superintendent in Father's place and Joseph his secretary, they had asked Peter to clerk for them. Guy's house was just a stone's throw from the Fort. If we were there, Peter would stay with us. I closed my eyes and prayed she'd say yes.

"My place is in my village," said Mother.

"Think of Peter. Stay nearby for a while, to please us both," John said. "Then we can think further on it."

Peter tried another tack. "The wagons will be going back empty when John and Lady Mary come up to the Hall, Mother. It's good economy for our things to go back to Fort Johnson in their wagons. And everything will be at hand to the river when the time comes to go to Canajoharie."

John looked pleased. "Well spoken, Peter, like a thrifty man of business!"

Mother looked down at her hands in her lap.

"Perhaps what you both say is best for now," she said at last. "But I do not intend to stay for long."

● ● ●

So it was decided. Betsy and Lana flew about as if it was a holiday we were going to, packing trunks and filling baskets and crates with our things.

Johnnie's wagons rumbled up the road to Johnson Hall laden with sideboards, credenzas, chests and chairs, a harpsichord and birdcages. When they were emptied, all our featherbeds, chairs and tables, trunks of silver and barrels of china were loaded in their stead. It made me feel odd to see them so out of place, setting off down the road.

When our rooms were near empty, Mother climbed into the carriage with Juba and Jenny and Baby Annie. We watched as she drew her shawl tight and turned her face from the house that Father had built for us. The horses clattered down the drive, Peter riding alongside on his roan mare. At the bend he turned back to wave. I tried to run after, but Lana caught my coat. Then Peggy poked me so hard I squealed.

"Why hurt Georgie, you horrible thing!" Lana cried.

"He only cares that Peter's home again!" Peggy burst into tears. "Can't he see we're losing the only home we know?"

Next morning the carriage returned for us and we left Johnson Hall for Fort Johnson. We wound down the path to the river, between the cornfields and cabins. Peggy sighed all the way, though Betsy tried to cheer her up.

"It will be different, but not so much as you fear. The Fort's much the same as the Hall."

"The Fort's *nothing* like the Hall! It's made of stone and the windows are small and the rooms dark and low."

Lana frowned at her, shaking her head at Mary and Susannah, meaning Peggy should not upset them.

"I suppose it's still a fine house, because Papa built it," Peg muttered with ill grace. "At least it's much bigger than Granny's."

"Are there swings?" Susannah asked.

"We'll make swings, Suky," Lana promised. "There's a stream for George hopping with frogs, and a millpond for eeling."

"And turtles?" asked Mary. "Will there be turtles?" She was very fond of the ones in the pond at the Hall.

"Big ones and little ones. And when winter comes we'll go sledding down the big hill."

"But I won't see my friends from school," Peg went on. "And we'll have to go so far to visit Johnstown. I think it will be very dull."

"You'll make fast friends at school at Fort Hunter," Betsy soothed. "The river's right at hand, so busy you cannot imagine. Boats come and go every day, with folks from Albany and New York always visiting. Nancy and Dan and Billy are close by, and Guy and Polly and the girls."

We passed a line of red-coat British soldiers marching along the road, muskets at their shoulders. Folk waved to us from horseback and wagons. Then we came in sight of the river and in hardly a minute drew up in front of Fort Johnson. The door opened, and there was Mother.

She was still in black, jet beads about her neck, but her face looked happier and her eyes weren't so red. She set Annie down and hugged us as if we'd been apart a month.

Inside were men with long brushes and buckets, distempering the walls. We dodged them, looking in all the rooms. And there were our own things, our chairs and chests and tables, laid out so it seemed like home, just as Betsy said. We went from one room to another, marveling how Mother had fixed it so. If here and there something was not right, Peggy moved it to her satisfaction.

Even the sleeping room looked the same as home. On the hooks were my spare shirt and breeches and my sisters' shifts and gowns. When I woke next morning the crows were cawing in the trees and sun was coming through the sycamore leaves. At first I thought I'd only dreamed we'd gone from Johnson Hall.

•••

At summer's end, when the cool weather came, Betsy and Lana were sent away to school in Schenectady. Peg begged to go with them, but Mother said ten was too young, and she couldn't be spared.

"It's all very well for you young ones," Peg complained. "But I must be eldest and do the household business and never play anymore."

It was true. Peg was at Mother's mercy, and my little sisters' chores were more like games. They helped in the kitchen, threading apple rings, braiding onion ropes and picking stones from the dried peas. For the rest they ran about with dolls or played at spindle-peg.

"And what do *you* do," Peg sniffed at me, "but fish and go frog-jigging in the marshes?"

"Fishing's work. And you'd best see to your sewing, or you'll have to do it over again." That made her flare, and I got out quick.

Boys did as they liked more than girls. I made new friends at the Fort Hunter school, and we roamed about as we pleased. I paddled with my Indian cousins or crossed to the landing to watch the boats. Some days the river was full from bank to bank with barges carrying crates of fowl and pigs, kegs of sherry, even apple trees and peach trees, wrapped and trussed, tall as me.

Once a crate landed that Father had ordered from

London before he died. Mother sent me to Guy's to fetch Peter and he galloped me back double. His eyes lit up smart when he saw the set of leather-bound books. There were music sheets too, rolled in oiled paper to protect them from the sea damp.

He was so eager to try the music that we had a concert that very night. Peter played the new English jigs on his fiddle, and my sisters skipped up and down the parlor. Mother sat in her straight chair, and I watched her foot tapping up and down. It seemed more like old times, except Father wasn't there.

I saw Peter every day, when he wasn't traveling. His work with Guy was so near he took some meals with us, and he mostly slept at home. Once the ducks and geese started south and the pigeons flocked, he got up early and tumbled me out of bed to go shooting.

"You're tall enough now to handle a short arm," he said, measuring me against his own musket barrel. "A couple of years yet before a long musket, though. You'd overbalance."

He gave me an old fowling piece that was his when he was young and a cartridge-pouch and horn all my own. When we brought home my first brace of ducks, he carried me whooping up the bank.

"A right keen eye, George Johnson! With a better piece, you'll be a crack shot before you're ten."

While Peter and I were off roaming, Mother set poor Peg to copying letters all day. When that was done, there was accounts of trade goods and rum to count up. Mother got cross if Peg made mistakes or mixed up the figures, saying Lana and Betsy would not have done so poorly.

"I daren't say it's because they had better schooling," Peggy said, out of her hearing. "I should keep accounts better if I was sent to Schenectady like them."

She wouldn't say so to Mother's face. Mother was short-tempered and stern with us for no reason. She still wore a black gown and jacket over her leggings and cried when-ever anyone spoke of Father. Sometimes she took to her room and we didn't see her for days.

But as time passed, she began to wear red or calico tunics and take more of an interest in our affairs. When Peter was about, he joked and made her laugh. She couldn't stay doleful, it wasn't her nature. She began keeping closer watch over the household, and let the servants know when the work was not done well.

And there was work aplenty, for we had no end of visi-tors. Chiefs and other travelers up and down the river came to tell their news and slept on our floor. Mother took their gifts of venison and bundled their furs and ginseng in the storeroom. She gave the Indians silver brooches and spoons and tobacco and told them what to say to Guy Johnson. She spent hours in the blockhouses checking supplies, readying for winter. We heard no more talk of going to Canajoharie.

Peggy still longed to go away to school. She pined for the company of Betsy and Lana and missed her friends in Johnstown. At last Mother gave in and said she might go study for the winter.

"I hope it will improve your ciphering, to say nothing of your disposition. George can count well enough for my needs while you're away, and more willingly."

But when Peg asked if she should have new shoes and gowns for town, Mother said she hadn't time to see to it. Peggy must ask Jenny and Juba and see what could be sewn up.

"So I did, but Lana and Betsy had the pick." Peggy looked sorrowful. "They had a trunk each with gowns and petticoats and jackets. And everything new — stockings and shifts and lovely calfskin shoes. There's only two calicos left and a linsey with turned sleeves and Lana's yellow silk made over. All I have new is slippers and a petticoat and a pocket from Nancy and a silk shawl from Polly. I'll be half-naked and shan't be able to show my face in town." On and on she went, but she still filled a big trunk with her things.

When the day came for her to go, Mother kissed her and told her to be good. Peter handed her into the boat. She looked so glad to be leaving. I thought how I would miss her, sharp tongue and all. She looked straight at me as if she knew and jumped up, catching Peter's arm.

"Let Georgie come with me to Schenectady. Can't he, Peter?"

"George is happy where he is," Peter said. And it was true. What made me sad was other people going away.

Later in the winter, when the river froze up, Peter went with some gentlemen in a cutter to visit Schenectady. He brought home news of my sisters, and the first letter to just myself in my whole life:

My Dearest Brother Georgy
I hope this finds you Well.
I am Well.

Peter has come yesterday and tells us of yr goings on up the Valley. It is most Pleasant to be in Schenectady. We stay in the brick house with Missus Brooks and go to school with Papa's nieces Susan and Anne Elizabeth. Susan says we needn't show our Mother is Mohawk for in the City what accounts is yr Father and ours was Sir William. So we are good as Ladies, tho my dress's are all two years out of date.

Peter says Mother will not keep in Fort Johnson once the ice has left. He talked to Betsy of Troubles in the Valley but I did not hear much of it. Anne Elizabeth says Peter is the handsom'st thing and wishes to know when he will come again.

Yr loving sister, Margaret Johnson

Peter roared with laughter at the last part. "I'll be certain to bow and smile at Mistress Anne Elizabeth when I do visit!"

Mother sent him in April to collect all three girls. She was set on going to Canajoharie and wanted us all together. When Peg asked if she should be allowed to go again, Mother said, "Schooling must wait for calmer times."

CANAJOHARIE

I CARRIED Peter's violin wrapped in oilskin in the canoe beside me. That way was safer than packed in a barrel with our things. "If you tip, hold it over your head till shore," he warned.

But the spring melt had passed and the water was low, so the journey to Canajoharie was easy paddling. I watched for the roof of Uncle Joseph's big barn. We turned in when we saw it, and there was Granny, waiting at the landing.

Our half-brothers Brant Johnson and William helped carry our bundles up the hill and through the palisades. We squeezed our trunks and boxes through the door, and I set Peter's violin on a shelf.

"Everything's tiny," cried Mary, looking about.

"Like a doll's house!" said Susannah.

Peg was blinking back tears. "However does she expect us to fit?"

Granny's house did seem small, after what we were used to. But it was still the biggest in the village, because Granny's husband had been chief. She had a front parlor and kitchen below, two sleeping rooms above, and a big Dutch fireplace to keep it all warm. The stairs were broad and wide, and made for extra sitting. But I couldn't slide down the handrail like I did at Johnson Hall, because it turned the corner too sharp.

Mother set me to line our chairs around every bit of wall. What wouldn't fit we carried to the new rooms for the servants. Then I thought I'd best stay out of the way. I started up the hill to Joseph's barn, but Granny spied me going, and said to take the horses out to graze. They came cantering across the fenced yard when they saw me — one dapple, the other near black.

The gray nudged me, and I went in the barn for the tethering ropes. It was the best barn for miles, with a loft and a ladder to it. I climbed up, and through a space between the boards I could see people going about their business and boats passing on the river. Inside all was dark and cool, the shadows full of rustling birds in the rafters.

I picked a pebble from the floor and took aim with my sling at a fat pigeon. The bright bars of sun coming in the cracks made it hard to see. But sudden, before I could let the shot go, the bird squawked and dived from its perch. It fell to the floor in a heap, feathers everywhere.

I had not yet even let fly!

I near jumped out of my skin. Was it bad magic, or a ghost spirit? I looked around in fear. But all I saw were wings above me as the other birds flapped in fright.

Then, in the light-striped shadows, something moved. The hair on my scalp rose higher. A dark head rose up behind the wagon. Then another poked up, and another. A figure ran from behind the wagon wheel and pounced on the pigeon at my feet.

"You'll have to be quicker than that!"

It was Sam Hill, shaking the bloody bird in my face. His own sling was in his hand.

The other boys came out and leapt on me and wrestled me to the ground, shouting and laughing. No ghosts — only my cousins! I tried to look like I hadn't been scared and knew it was them all along.

Sam let me up. "We knew you was coming," he said. Then he stuck his face by mine. "Now that Degonwadonti's come to live here, will Thayendanegea come back too?"

I shook my head. I did not think Uncle Joseph would be returning soon. Guy Johnson kept him so much on Department business that we'd hardly even seen him at Fort Johnson.

Sam waited for me to speak. When I did not, he held up the pigeon, limp in his hand. "Want to try for another?"

A few swallows swooped around the barn, but there was no meat on them. "They're frighted now."

"Not here — along the creek."

The dapple-gray stuck his head in the door and snorted. He was still waiting for his feed. "Granny says I'm to tether the horses in the fields. And I haven't et since daybreak."

Sam's brother Tom was already reaching the ropes down from their hooks. "We'll take the horses," he said over his shoulder. "You can follow."

I tore away to the house, and Cato cut me some bread and pork in the back kitchen.

"What's your hurry, boy?" he called as I ran out again. I followed the hoof marks across the fields, and caught up with the others by the trout pool. The horses were grazing, the boys lined up on a log in the sun.

Sam waved me over. I hadn't even caught my breath when he began plaguing me again for news of Joseph.

"He travels about," I said. "I don't know where."

Another boy nodded. "We know. He goes to talk with all the tribes. He knows the mind of Guy Johnson. Will Thayendanegea get us guns to drive out the whites who take our hunting grounds?"

Some Dutch boys were sitting along the log too, and I thought they wouldn't like to hear such talk. But one spoke up.

"Pa says our grandpap bought our farm fair and square from Terihoga Brant. These rabble should do the same. Buy it, like us. Not steal it."

They looked to me again and waited. But even if I knew what was in the mind of Guy Johnson and the other gentlemen, I couldn't tell them. Mother said we must keep counsel and never say to others what we heard.

"Why has Degonwadonti come here?" pressed Tom. "Why has she left the fine houses of the British?"

"To be near our grandmother and her people. She says it is safer at Canajoharie, now we don't have Father to make the white folk behave."

"It will be safer yet when Thayendanegea returns and calls the braves together," said Tom.

●●●

Next day Mother sent me and Peg and Mary to the village

school. Betsy and Lana were too old to go, and Susannah and Annie too young. There were near thirty scholars, some Mohawk, some white, and us in the middle. Schoolmaster McConnel was from Albany, but we knew him from before. He had lessoned us once at Fort Hunter.

Life went on. And it was not very different from down the Valley. What was unlike was we spoke Mohawk as much as English now. I learned to speak a little Seneca and some Onondaga — at least "Good morning," or "Would you like to eat?" — because when we came downstairs for breakfast there were often travelers sleeping on the floor, just as in our other houses. And to the adults in the village, we answered to our new name, Children of Degonwadonti.

Mother and Granny kept up Joseph's old store. They took in furs and ginseng roots and traded them for rum and kettles. And they sold sewing from the women in the village — deerskin shirts and leggings and moccasins. My older sisters were set to work embroidering, and Betsy's work was fine and much sought after. Peg said she would do a whole dress, but she didn't ever finish it.

There were many whites to trade with, as folk from Johnstown had lately bought farms near our village. The Dyggerts were there when we came, and Caty Dyggert was glad to see Peggy again. She sat by Peg at school and fancied herself my sister's dearest companion, though Peg called her coarse and greedy. Still they spent much time together, falling out and making up. Caty always begged to try on Peg's gowns, but Peg said no.

I wished Peter lived with us, but he stayed on at Fort

Johnson and only rode down on Sundays. I wanted to tell him about new colts and litters of hound pups and other news, but his visits were taken up with talking to Mother. All during the week he wrote up Guy's reports to the governor. On Sundays he'd pass on to her what they said, and she'd pass it on to the chiefs as she thought fit.

The third time he visited, it was a rainy afternoon. Mother sat, but Peter walked about or stoked the fire. They talked about the border raids.

"It's worsening," Peter said.

Mother nodded. "News comes to me each day. There are ever more clashes. The whites stop where they like, and build what they want. No title, nor deed, and William's treaty goes for nothing."

Her voice was angry, but also sad. "They spoil the hunting grounds, so many cannot even feed their families. Guy *must* take action to stop it. The Cayuga say they cannot hold the young braves much longer."

Peter poked the logs. "Guy is planning a new conference at Oswego. That may help."

"It will only stir up trouble. He's playing to the warriors, not the peacemakers."

"Thousands are coming this time," Peter said proudly. "Guy says it's the biggest ever. Bigger even than the last — " He stopped short. He didn't say "when Father died," but I could see he had meant to.

"Your father would not have waited this long. He would have seen the anger rising. He would have gone directly to the council fires. More of our people each day call the elders to raise war parties."

"You will go to Oswego, won't you, Mother?" Peter asked. "Guy wishes you to."

She looked toward the river. "No. I have been to many conferences. This one will make no difference. So Guy is going, and Joseph, of course, and Dan. Who else?"

All the gentlemen, Peter said. Mr. Chew and Dr. Dease. And Mr. Tice. And all the officers and men of the Department.

Mother raised her eyebrows. "So many, for only a conference. Joseph says that Nancy and Polly and the children go too. And why, I wonder?"

Peter stabbed at the fire until the sparks flew.

"I think you have more to tell me, son," she pressed him. "This 'conference' hides something."

Peter turned round in astonishment. "How do you know?"

"Joseph has let me know something of it. And I have ears."

My brother looked round the room, though no one was there but my sisters and me. "There's talk some may go on up to Canada after the council," he said in a low voice.

Betsy put down her sewing. Peggy's mouth was an O.

"Fleeing the Valley!" Mother said with scorn. "Dan is a coward."

"He is not, Mother," Peter said quickly. "Blood was let in Boston just ten days past. The rabble are arming. Seventy-three King's soldiers shot down! But all the rebels think of is their own Yankee blood on the Concord grass. They want revenge. And ... and there've been threats ... against Guy and John."

"Threats?"

"They say they'll take Guy and put him away, if he doesn't join them. What use is he to the King in prison, or dragged out and hung!"

Guy, hung? What did Peter mean?

"Mother, come with us, please," he urged. "The Valley is no longer safe for any Johnson."

Betsy leaned forward. "Are you in danger, Peter?"

"No, Betsy." He shook his head. "Guy maintains the garrison, and we still have our arms. But there's Yankee spies everywhere. They're trying to stir up the farmers and village folk against us. Rabble march past every day."

"It is just a show," said Mother. "They've nothing to do but play at soldiering."

"I know," said Peter. "They can't drill, they can't form ranks, they've no proper arms. Yet more of them strut about all the time."

"Guy is weak. Does he think the name of your father counts for so little, dead less than a year? John is not leaving."

"No, John will stand fast. He has his Highlanders to protect him, and he stays on civil terms with old friends, even those who've turned rebel. It's you I fear for," said Peter, looking at her direct. "And my sisters and George."

"I will protect us." She answered calmly, folding her arms. "I am among my own people. And I do not wish to be part of Guy's exodus. I have properties and business to look after. And you, son. Will you go up to Canada with the others?"

Peter answered so quick, I could tell he'd made up his mind. "I'd go to fight for the King, Mother. If I have your blessing."

"No!" She spoke sharp and reached to catch his arm. "No. You must stay here! We will not be driven from our home."

Peter looked anxious. "Do you forbid me to go, Mother?"

No one breathed. The silence stretched so I wished I could run from the room.

But then she dropped her hand from his arm. When she spoke again, it was in quite another way. "I know what is in your mind. At the same age Joseph went with your father to Niagara to fight. John did as well. I do not trust Guy's judgment, but if the treaties are to hold, he must put a stop to this foolishness. And it's only King's men will keep the settlers from taking more of our land."

This speech seemed to change something. She straightened in her chair. "Your father would have you go where you are needed. Go, then — but not for long. I cannot manage without you."

Peter kissed her and put on his hat, and left to go back down the river. The servants cleared away the tea, and everyone started speaking at once.

Why was everyone leaving? I asked. When would they be coming back? And where on earth was Canada?

But Mother only said, "They'll return when this is settled."

Peggy said I should put the talk about leaving out of my mind.

"Don't think or speak of it, and it might not happen," she said.

She was wrong.

●●●

"Boats on the river! Boats on the river!" I heard shouts coming from the landing.

Juba caught me by my breeches as I ran for the door. "It's the folk going up to Oswego. Your mam says to put on your good shirt."

By the time I'd grabbed my shirt and run to the river the first canoes were already around the bend. Then I could see a line of bateaux, and scows, flatboats and skimmers. More and more came on, strung out down the river till I couldn't see an end to it. The ducks took to the air squawking as the paddlers and oarsmen stroked against the current. Some folk were singing, and they waved and called out to us on the landing. Mother was in her best clothes, my sisters in white. It was like a fair day, except some of the faces were sad and scared.

Brant Johnson and some others launched canoes from our bank and paddled out to greet Uncle Joseph. I looked for Peter, and spied him in one of the big boats near the front with Guy and Dan. Our half-sisters Polly and Nancy Claus were in another boat with Polly's girls and Billy Claus. I saw Mr. Tice, the tavern-keeper, and some Butlers, and Old Frey, and mad Yost, and the Murrays and McKays and McDonells. It seemed like every person I knew in my whole life passed on the river that day — all but us, and John and Lady Mary, who were staying firm at Johnson Hall.

Our family canoes turned in at the wharf as Cato and Jenny hurried down with baskets of corn cakes and roast meat, cold barley water and hot tea. I ran to meet Peter, but Mother called me back.

"Help Polly Johnson to the house."

Polly's face was red as flannel, and she clutched her belly. Peg whispered to me that the baby inside was almost ready to be born.

"Thank you, George," gasped Polly and took my arm. She leaned on me so heavy that I staggered. Her little girls climbed the hill behind us, the youngest one in the maid-servant's arms.

"This is no time to travel," Mother scolded her. She poured out a bowl of tea as Polly sank with a groan into a chair. "Your father would have forbid it. He kept me close to home at my times."

Polly tried to get her breath. "Molly, do you think I would have chosen to leave when I should be taking to my bed? If Father was alive, none of us would be going from our homes today." She blew on her tea and drank some. "My other babies came easy. Pray the Lord this one will too."

Peter and Uncle Joseph ducked in through the door. They were dressed alike in blue cloth coats, and Peter was near as tall as Joseph. Mother took Joseph aside and they bent their heads in the corner.

Peter caught up Mary and Susannah and Baby Anne in turn and kissed and tickled them and made them laugh. He shook my hand and ruffed my hair.

"Don't look so sad, Georgie. Who says I won't be back in time for the fall shooting? We'll get up early like we used to. Now, mind you don't go fishing for pike without me to help you land it!"

But I stuck to his hand and wouldn't let go.

"Take me too," I cried. "Take me too! I can shoot."

The words came out in a squeak. Everyone turned to stare.

Mother was across the room in two steps. Her fingers closed on my shoulders, pulling me away from Peter. I stared up into her angry face.

"No! Do not speak of going. You're only a child."

I looked back at Peter, but he nodded, his smile gone. "You're hardly eight, George. This isn't your campaign. Not yet."

Uncle Joseph loosed Mother's hands and stood me upright. He knelt and kept his arm around my shoulders and spoke to me, but his eyes were on Mother. "There'll be time enough for shooting when we return. And pray then it be deer. I have no stomach to hunt my neighbors."

Peter looked from Mother to me. "God willing, this business will be settled quickly. Until then you must be the man, George, and look out for the family for me."

Joseph slapped me on the back. "Listen to your brother, George. You must watch all these womenfolk." His face spread in a grin. "Peter's right. All may yet be well, and we'll take you on the fall hunt when we return."

But Mother stood like stone and did not speak. Peter went and put his arms about her.

"Mother," he said quietly, "give me your kiss. We may not see each other for some little time."

She held him tight for a moment, her head against his. Then she stepped back and let her arms fall. "God go with you," she said in Mohawk.

The boats set out again. I ran along the muddy bank, shouting and waving, tears flying off my face.

The last sight I had of Peter, he was in the stern of the bateau, smiling and waving back as if he was off on a jaunt. Then the river took him out of my view.

"Polly's dead."

I stopped carving my sling and stared up at Peggy.

"Polly's *dead*." She spoke louder this time, hoarse. The freckles on her face stood out clear enough to count.

"How do you know?"

She nodded toward the kitchen. "I heard. The babe that was to be born died too." She whirled and ran off.

Mother was in the same chair where Polly had rested. Her head was in her hands.

"Aieeehh," she moaned. "I knew it would not go well. I saw it in her face, poor soul. A year to the day her father was taken from us."

"W-what will happen to her little girls?" Betsy stammered.

"Poor things." Mother rocked in her chair and groaned. "Poor souls, poor souls."

Granny pulled her shawl over her head and started a keening wail. Mother joined in. Their cries filled up the room and I fled back out.

Betsy came stumbling behind me out the door. A few steps on, she fell down in a heap.

I crouched by her and she wet my shirt with her tears. "Oh, George," she wailed, "nothing's been right since Papa left us."

I thought about Polly leaning on my arm on the path to our house. Good-hearted Polly, who played with my little sisters and always brought me sweets when she came to visit. Now she was gone too, like Father.

"When will Peter come back?" I asked. But Betsy only shook her head and didn't answer.

The elders had come back from the conference and told Mother what happened. Nothing had gone well. All the gifts and speeches had not calmed the anger over the treaty lands. Guy's heart was not in the speaking, they said, because Polly had sickened and died on the way to Oswego.

No one talked of anything but Polly and Guy. What had happened to Peter? I had to listen a long time at doors and in the kitchen before I learned he'd gone up to Canada with the others from the Valley.

"They'll fight in the King's service there till the troubles pass here," said Abram.

"What troubles?" I asked.

He shook his head in sorrow. "White folks' troubles."

●●●

For many weeks we had no more word at all. Finally in August a runner brought letters. Mother gave them to Betsy to read out.

"Two of them are from Peter, George!" She scanned them quick. "He says he's well."

They'd waited for weeks and weeks at Oswego for boats to fetch them to Montreal, Peter said. But when they got there, the troubles had arrived too. All the Valley men were made soldiers at once.

"*I have joined Butler's Rangers,*" he wrote, "*with the rank of lieutenant. Walter Butler is the same. I'm proud to be his equal, for he's a good man.*"

"Peter an officer!" said Mother, amazed. "If John Butler is company colonel, it's easy for his son to get a rank. But Peter's hardly sixteen."

Tavern-keeper Mr. Tice was to be their captain, and Uncle Joseph was a captain too, with his own company. Everyone was getting uniforms to fight for the King.

Indeed, Peter's second letter told us, they had fought already!

"*We crushed the Rebels in a skirmish to the south at St. John's — the Blue-Coats ran, but poor Captain Tice is badly wounded in the foot and cannot march. Mohawk Captain Daniel was killed.*"

Mother had Betsy gather my sisters and the servants to pray for God to protect Peter and Uncle Joseph and Captain Tice. She sent blankets and an ax head to comfort Captain Daniel's family.

I didn't know who Peter was fighting. Rebels, he said. And blue-coats. The troops that marched back and forth on the far bank of the river wore blue coats — those who had coats to wear. They never did us harm. They paddled across to trade, lifting their caps to Lana and Betsy and smiling as they bargained. Mother sold them soap or tobacco or rum as they wished. Were they a different sort of blue-coats from the ones Peter wrote about?

Uncle Joseph and Peter had worn blue coats, standing in our parlor. Would folk think them rebels too, and fire at them?

Abram and Cato laughed at me when I asked. "They'll have tossed off them farmers' coats for Ranger's green by now."

"Not red coats, like Guy and Father?"

"No. They ain't regular army. They's Rangers, Valley people. Best fighters ever was — won the French war, they did. Don't need a red coat to make a proper soldier," said Cato.

•••

In the cold of November another letter came from Peter. What a letter that was! The rebels had come right up to Montreal. A Vermonter named Ethan Allen had raised troops and crossed the mountains to Lake Champlain and captured great Fort Ticonderoga. He was set to take Canada when my own brother stopped them. Peter himself had taken the rebel colonel's sword!

Captain Crawford of the 26th held the Rebels in check until Walter and I arrived with 30 Rangers — and as many Indians. The Vermonters took shelter in a barn, but we turned their own field piece upon them — flushed them out like rats, and they ran toward us. Walter fired his pistol but missed. Col. Allen fired back, but wide. I pursued him with my pistol drawn, crying at him to Surrender or he is a Dead Man.

"If treated with Honor, I shall," he shouts. So I moved to take his sword, and at that a Seneca dashed betwixt us, hoping to split Col. Allen's skull with his Tomahawk. The giant Vermonter grabbed me and whirled me between him and his Attacker. But the Seneca flyed round with great Fury, trying to single out his enemy without scalping me. Then another Seneca darts forward, and yet another, until Allen is twitching me round with such velocity the world blurs before my eyes — I believed I was back dancing in Peggy's arms at Johnson Hall!

At last up comes Sergeant O'Connor with fixed bayonet and swears by Jasus he will kill every one of the Fiends. With poor grace the Indians fall back. After that 'tis all arranged. With Lt. Butler on one side of Allen, and Captain Crawford and one of the French noblesse on the other, we stroll along to the gates of Montreal. Col. Allen gives us news of Ticonderoga. I like him very well — for a rebel villain.

In a few weeks he is to be escorted to London to be hanged. Guy and Dan sail on the same ship, to ask the King for troops and money for the war. Uncle Joseph goes also, to pray the Nations and their Allies can hope for permanent protection against the tide of settlement.

And I — think of it — am to sail with them! I am to get a commission from the King, as reward for the service of capturing Col. Allen. Some say they should make me a general, but I'll be satisfied with any rank, knowing little enough of generaling.

Betsy lifted her head in amazement. "He's going to England, Mama. To London!"

"To London," Mother said faintly. "What else does he say? When does he return?"

Betsy looked back to the close-written pages. "They'll sail for home in spring. '*Send word quick to let me know what you wish me to bring you*,'" he says.

"Sleeves," Peggy said. "Like the ones in *Modes de Paris*. And a mantelet with fur tippets."

"Real books," said Lana. "The plays of Master Shakespeare — John kept Father's set. And *The Adventures of Roderick Random* that Father used to read us."

Mary wanted butterflies for her collection, and Susannah asked for a doll with a real china head. Annie was old enough to talk now and said she wanted one too.

Mother ordered fruit trees — greengages and peaches like those Father had planted at Johnson Hall. She kept shaking her head as if she couldn't believe her ears.

"Taking a ship to London — a commission from the King! If only his father had lived to know it. Just sixteen and abroad in the world!" She took the letter and put it with all the others, in a box that Father gave her with a pearly lid.

Betsy took out paper and quill. "What do you want from London, Georgie? You're the only one who has not said."

But I didn't want anything. Peter was crossing the sea to get his red coat. He'd promised he'd be home for fall shooting, and now he was going to London, without a word to me to say he was sorry of it.

●●●

Winter came and went. When the ice left, another letter arrived from Peter to say he'd been with Guy and Dan and

Joseph to the royal palace to see the King. His Majesty had promised help for our people.

So why didn't Joseph return home? my cousins asked.

"He should come back and tell us how the King will help us," said Sam Hill. "Who but Thayendanegea will save our lands? The elders will not fight. They say the Mohawk should not join the white quarrels, but it was red-coats that kept the squatters off our lands. Who will do so now?"

For we hardly saw a red-coat anymore. It seemed like all of them had left when the Valley folk went up the river. More and more blue-coats took their place — a few at first, then full companies. Patrols marched into our village and went among the houses of the white folk, looking for boys to join their new Continental army. Caty Dyggert told Peg her ma had asked the soldiers in, to see if there was pay involved.

"I told her it was most disloyal, and we would never do so," Peggy said. "Of course you're too young, George, and they wouldn't take you. But Caty's ma said loyal goes with custom, and there's no custom when your neighbors have all stolen away in the night."

That was more true all the time. One night Sir John went too.

For a year after the others left, John stayed on in the Valley to see to his tenants and his farms. Then Mother learned from her spies that the rebel Colonel Schuyler was marching with troops from Albany to arrest him. She sent a runner with a warning, and John fled the Hall that same night with his house guard and all his Highlanders and some families too.

Lady Mary bravely stayed behind to make the rebels think John was still at home. When Colonel Schuyler found out, he was so mad he arrested her and the babies and took them away to Albany in a carriage. His soldiers gave chase upriver, but they missed John and the rest entirely. John didn't take the river route but led them right over the mountains. A terrible journey it was. Most reached Montreal, but some starved and died. The mothers and little children had the worst of it.

And that left us the only Johnsons in the Valley.

•••

One day in summer two young Dutch soldiers stopped at our house and asked for Mrs. Brant. Their new blue uniforms were too small, and they tugged at their sleeves as they waited. When Betsy fetched Mother, they told her the Continentals were holding a conference, upriver at German Flats.

Would Mother come? they asked. The Oneida and Tuscarora would be there, and many Mohawk.

Mother folded her arms. "For what purpose?"

"We want to correct the lies the British have told," one said, like a speech he'd practiced. "They're no longer friends to the Indians. The way of your people lies with true Americans."

"General Washington will be generous with his gifts," the other promised.

Mother bowed her head. "I will consider my duty as a clan mother and inform my people."

They looked from one to the other, not sure if she'd agreed to come. The first pressed on. "And ... your brother,

Chief Joseph Brant ... our captain wishes to know how we may convey the invitation to him."

"My brother, Captain Brant, has gone to London."

She said good-day to them and went inside.

"But I would like to know who is coming to this conference of theirs," she said to Granny. "I intend to discover what they want of Joseph." She put on a good calico gown and black-edged blanket and walked out with Betsy and Lana and me.

Spying some men in the shade of an elm at the crossroads, she made straight for them. "I see our neighbors Farmer Wagner and Farmer Herkimer have joined the rebels," she murmured to us. Another soldier was with them and a fourth man in a preacher's coat.

"Good day, neighbors. I see you are become soldiers — officers, no less," she said.

Farmer Herkimer chewed his pipestem and made no answer. He was Father's old friend who lived down the river in a big brick house near as fine as Johnson Hall. Though he had joined the Continentals, I heard one of his sons had gone up to Canada with Peter to fight for the British.

Farmer Wagner bowed a little toward us. "Mrs. Brant, out walking with your pretty daughters! Pray may I introduce Colonel Tench Tilghman, secretary and aide-de-camp to General George Washington."

Colonel Tilghman bowed too and smiled at Mother and my sisters. He was handsome and his uniform was splendid, with gold buttons. He had a short sword hung at his hip.

"I've heard much about you, Mrs. Brant. I hope you will

be coming to our conference. General Washington himself sends his special regards to you and to your brother. He remembers Joseph well from their early travels together. Please tell your brother so."

"Alas," said Mother, "my brother has been gone from the Valley for more than a year."

"I hope he will return soon. General Washington knows the great influence he and yourself have with your people. Your presence at the conference would be of great value."

Mother smiled back without speaking. Then she turned to the man in the dark coat.

"Reverend Kirkland," she said, "I must charge you with neglect for not calling upon me."

I was surprised she spoke so mild. Father had cursed Mr. Kirkland as a two-faced villain, though he was the missionary to the Oneida. "Sam Kirkland is no end of trouble," he'd said. "He uses his cloth to preach against the King, and there's money behind him, every step."

I could see no money behind him, only worn coat-tails, and on top of his greasy queue his hair was quite thin.

"There was a time when you were often in my husband's house," Mother chided him. "Perhaps you fear you will not be accommodated in comfort or the company will be dull. We have so little news here."

His face flushed dark. "That is not what I hear, madam," he snapped. "Some say you are well informed indeed. John Johnson would say so, I think."

Farmer Herkimer took his pipe from his mouth and cleared his throat to change the talk. "Molly, I fear ye are thinner. Have ye been ill?"

"If I am reduced, sir, it is not through sickness." Her handkerchief went to her eyes. "It is the remembrance of a loss that can never be made up." She took Betsy's arm and walked on. Colonel Tilghman and Farmer Wagner tipped their hats. Farmer Herkimer and Reverend Kirkland stood watching as we left.

She'd told them nothing and got news from them instead!

"They wish to recruit Joseph and me for the rebel cause," she told Granny when we got home. "Washington's sent his pretty ambassador to woo us. But the honey talk won't hold. Washington doesn't like the Indians."

"Joseph's reputation is growing," said Granny.

"If they can't win him over, they'll hunt him down," warned Mother.

Next afternoon three Continentals knocked at our door.

"Oh, we know them!" Peg sang out, peering through the upstairs window. "One is Minna Henry's brother from Johnstown."

"Whatever can they want?" Lana asked.

I heard Juba speak high and excited to Mother in the parlor. "The gentlemen are asking to pay their respects to the Miss Johnsons."

Mother said back, "Tell them the Miss Johnsons are not up."

"But, Miss Molly, it's one o'clock!" Juba said, scandalized.

"Then they would be fools not to take my meaning. I will not have my daughters called upon by rebels."

And Juba sent them away.

"But we know them from Johnstown," Peggy cried. "It's

Jeb Henry, Minna's brother who had the bay horse and
trap!"

Lana told her to hush. "Mother won't like to hear you
talk so."

Peggy knew better than to say a word to Mother, but she
wrote MRS MARGARET HENRY in her copybook to spite
her. Betsy caught her at it and made her scratch it out.

"What would Peter think if he saw you?" she scolded.
"He risks his life fighting the rebels, and you'd have us
entertain them in our mother's house?"

Peg looked shamed but wouldn't say so. "They're only
boys dressed as soldiers. Mother said we should be man-
nerly to them when they come to trade. Besides, she has
Captain Bloomfield to tea and he is a Continental."

It was true Captain Bloomfield had come twice to call
on Mother. He was like Colonel Tilghman, the gentle-man-
nered sort of rebel. He asked most politely to buy deerskin
moccasins and leggings to send to his sisters in the East.
"Your young ladies are very kind to make such things for
me," he said, making a fuss of Betsy's embroidery. Juba
baked him honey biscuits.

"Mother lets him call because she wants the news from
Johnstown," said Betsy. "The captain's troops are quar-
tered at Johnson Hall, under direct orders of General
Washington."

"There are still some furnishings left, much as you
would remember, ma'am," he told Mother. Captain
Bloomfield threw out the rabble who'd been camping there
since John had gone to Canada.

"The Hall is under my personal protection. Though I am

sorry to say my own men took down wampum belts from the fireplace, hoping to sell them. I had them whipped, Mrs. Brant, I assure you."

•••

More of our Indian relatives were leaving the village all the time, going west where the hunting was still good. Sam and Tom Hill's family sold up and moved nearer Seneca lands. Mother said it was a shame how the white settlers got Indian farms so cheap. "A few dollars for fine wood houses and all the crops and orchards!"

She spoke angrily to the clan matrons and tried to make them speak out to stop people selling to the whites. "These white families care little for the King. Their numbers are growing every day while we grow fewer. How can we guard the Eastern Door, as our ancestors did?"

"But what can we do?" one shrugged as she ate the food Mother set before her. "The British have left us."

"That is *not* so," said Mother. "Bide your time and stay loyal. Thayendanegea will return, and Guy Johnson, and they will bring soldiers with them and take the Valley back from the rebels."

An old one scowled. "The whites are like greedy dogs. They have so much and always want more. This fight is like the last one, between the French and British. When brothers fight each other, who knows who will win?"

"There is no doubt who will win." Mother's eyes flashed in the candlelight. "The rebels have no King, no proper army, no money."

She said the Mohawk must never be like the treacherous Oneida who had broken the Covenant Chain and gone to the rebel side. The Mohawk must remember their great friend Sir William and their great protector the King.

But with so many Mohawk gone west, our school was mostly white children now. One day in the yard Giles Ten Brock threw a stone that landed at my feet. I shied it back, thinking it was a game.

"Damn Tory!" he yelled. Only a week before we had gone hunting duck eggs together.

I laughed, uncertain. No one had called me "damn" before. He threw another stone that hit me on the cheek.

I felt the place where the stone struck, but no blood showed on my fingers. Others gathered around us in a circle.

"Don't look at me, I'm not your friend!" Giles shouted. He knocked me down and ran away, bawling, "Damn Tory! Damn Indian!" at the top of his lungs.

~ 6 ~
ORISKANY

VOICES roused me in the dark, so early not even the
birds were awake. One voice was Mother's.

I was on the stairs and tiptoeing down in the candlelight
when I saw the red coat.

Peter?

The red coat turned — silver at his throat, white eagle
feathers glowing in his scalplock. Uncle Joseph!

His arms went around my shivering shoulders, the
rough wool smelling of smoke, gunpowder and grease. His
lips brushed my cheek.

Mother rose and took me from him. "George, back to
bed," she said, quiet but meaningful. "Leave us now."
From the shadows Joseph smiled at me and put a finger to
his lips.

In my bed I tried to listen, but their voices were low. I
must have slept, for I heard nothing more. In the morning
there was no sign of him.

No, Betsy said, I had not dreamt him. But I must not
breathe a word of it to anyone. Joseph had come back

across the sea, and Peter too. They had helped take back
New York from the rebels. There had been plenty of fighting, but the King had sent ships and an army, and the
rebels had finally fled.

Are we safe here now? I asked.

New York was safe, she said, but not the country, not
yet. There were still rebels in Albany, and New Jersey, and
we must be careful. Joseph had made his way home in
secret through enemy lines.

"No one must know he's back, George. Mind you don't
speak of it."

"And Peter?"

She shook her head. "Peter stays east with his regiment,
now he is an officer."

●●●

Some days after, a big man on a white horse stopped at our
gate.

"Good-day to ye, Molly Brant," he roared out. Mother
came from the store to speak with him.

"What do you want, Farmer Herkimer?" she asked. She
stared up and down at his blue uniform. "Or it is *General*
Herkimer now?"

"What news of Joseph?" he barked, not even taking his
pipe from his yellow teeth.

"No news, Nicolas. You know he went to England to
petition the King."

I did not blink. Betsy had said no one must know Joseph
was back.

"And has returned, I hear," Herkimer said.

"You hear more than I do."

He scowled and pointed his pipe stem at her. "I've come to warn ye, Molly, it's time ye left the Valley. I can protect yer family no longer."

Behind him two young soldiers lined up along the fence, their horses cropping the grass. They looked into the yard at Lana and Peggy feeding guinea fowls, and took off their hats. Peggy bade them good-day, though Lana did not.

"What do you mean, Nicolas?" asked Mother.

"I mean they'll be coming to take ye and yer lot away to Albany. Like they did Lady Mary Johnson." He mopped his face, which ran with sweat in the sun. His horse switched its long white tail against the rails.

"Why should I leave this place, Nicolas?" she answered, her voice firm. "My family is here. I have this store to tend. My tenants are always needful. They will be more so when your troops begin to take our winter supplies."

He leaned down toward her, his saddle creaking. "The whole Valley knows it was you warned John to go that night. Ye've got runners up and down the road to Canada, Molly, carrying tales of our doings to that devil, Guy Johnson."

Mother laughed. "Where do you hear such things, Nicolas? Spying? Is that Oneida girl who warms your bed making herself useful?"

"Blast ye, woman! That's none of yer affair!"

The soldiers behind him grinned.

"I do not wish to leave my people, Nicolas. Sir William's many *true* friends will see no harm comes to us. I wish only peace and good harvests as we once had, and the swift return home of my son."

"Acchh," he growled, shaking his head at her. "It's beyond that now, woman. Yer Nations have no one to protect them. Yer William's long gone. Those sweet days are done for us all."

Herkimer grunted and raised his hand to his soldiers. I watched them as they rode off, but Mother had long since turned her back.

●●●

A few weeks later, on a wet night in August, all the warriors left the village.

After they'd gone, Mother was at the store from early in the morning until long after dark, talking and talking. Runners came and went. Sometimes she wrote letters in Mohawk. Sometimes my sisters wrote for her in English. More often, for safety, the runners carried her meaning only in their minds.

If visitors came late at night, she brought them in the house and I overheard their talk. But no one told me direct what was happening. I listened to Juba and Cato whispering in the kitchen and Betsy and Lana at their sewing, and I pieced it out.

There was to be a great battle to end the war and bring everyone back to the Valley!

Guy Johnson was coming from Montreal with a British general and many red-coats. Everyone who'd gone away to Canada was coming back to fight. Sir John was bringing his own regiment, the Royal Greens, and Dan Claus was coming, and John Butler was bringing the Rangers. Uncle Joseph would lead his own company, and the tribes. Our warriors had gone upriver to meet them at Oswego.

They were going to take back Fort Stanwix, up in Oneida territory. Beyond the fort was all our Indian land, by Father's treaty. Our lands would be safe when the King held the fort again. Only a few blue-coats were holding it, and they were untried in battle. It would be an easy victory.

But after the warriors left, Mother got word General Herkimer had found out about the battle. He was moving his blue-coats along the river road. Hundreds of our neighbors were joining them, marching west with the army to relieve the fort!

At once she sent for a swift runner to warn Uncle Joseph. She looked frightened. So were we all.

"Don't breathe a word of it," Juba cautioned me. "We don't know who's with us and who's aginst."

General Herkimer's own son was fighting with the British, we heard. But then some loyals had relatives who'd gone over to the rebel side too. If anyone got wind of Mother's warning, the blue-coats could hear of it.

"And we'll all be killed, you hear me?" Juba drew her finger across her throat like a knife.

The clan mothers were not happy that their men had gone to battle. Mother went among them, calming and persuading. She said once the British had the fort, they'd push the blue-coats out and take back our Valley for the King. The war would be finished and all the Johnsons would come back home. The greedy squatters would be made to give back the land they'd taken, and we would have our hunting grounds again.

I listened, but I worried. What would happen if General Herkimer found out it was Mother who spoiled his fight?

Five nights after the warriors left, I dreamed a terrible dream. I was on a field, with bare trees, and fog rising, or smoke, so I couldn't see. Everything was still and quiet, except for a crow squawking.

I saw people lying on the plowed ground, half-hidden by the mist. I looked at them, though I didn't want to. I knew they were dead.

Then I saw a red-coat off by himself, curled up with his back to me. The fog lifted up, and it was Peter. He wasn't wounded, just tired and still, with his eyes looking up to the sky. I called and called his name, but he didn't seem to see me. I couldn't make him see me.

Peg shook me awake. "Shush, Georgie! How can I sleep with you thrashing so?"

"I dreamed about Peter."

"Go back to sleep," she said. But for a long time I shook with fear and couldn't get the mist from my mind.

At breakfast I blurted out to Betsy and Lana, "Is Peter at the fighting?"

They looked at me in surprise over their tea, then at each other.

"We shouldn't speak of it, George," said Betsy. "You know that." She hesitated, then said, low, "But you know he's not with the others. He's in Philadelphia, with his regiment."

"In Philadelphia, for certain?"

"Yes. The 26th regiment is there with General Howe, freeing the city."

"We're sure to have a letter any day," said Lana.

"Or he'll be home," I said. "Soon as the war's won."

•••

Two days later the warriors filed back into the village. Some of the younger braves were claiming victory, strutting and crowing, blue coats turned inside out over their bare shoulders, fresh scalps hanging from their belts. But many were limping and crusted with blood.

Some did not come back at all.

Awful cries came from the Indian houses. I kept close to home and waited for news.

The elders came straight to speak to Mother. They'd only gone along to watch the British victory, saying we should leave the whites to fight themselves. Now their faces were streaked with black in mourning, their eyes rimmed with red.

One elder named Nickus spat on the road. "So many deaths. Brother fighting brother. The Great Peace broken! And for what? The red-coats didn't even take the fort!"

Mother's hand went to her face. "Did my warning not reach Joseph?"

"It did." Nickus took his rum from her hand and drank it down. "When Thayendanegea heard Herkimer's troops were marching, he made an ambush at Oriskany Creek. The Oneida ran like women."

But he did not seemed pleased.

"Clan against clan. Seneca against Oneida, Tuscarora fighting Mohawk." He made a disgusted sound. "So many warriors of noble blood slain — and the hairs of the British scarcely ruffled."

There was no honor in the fighting, the elders said, only

tricks. A spy the British captured told them a lie that General Benedict Arnold was marching to relieve the fort with an army of rebel troops thousands strong — "As many as leaves on the trees!" Nickus said.

So the red-coats stopped their siege and fled all the way back to Oswego.

"They were fools."

There was more disgrace. As the warriors fought Herkimer at the creek, the blue-coat general Willett came out of the fort and ransacked the Indian camp. "They shamed us. Took all we had. We came home without our shirts, without our blankets."

"How many of our people lost?"

"Thirty. Many Seneca, fewer Mohawk."

"Who?" Mother whispered. "Which clans?"

They said out the names. Joseph was safe. But our brother William of Canajoharie was killed.

Mother started. "No! He is not dead."

Nickus said he saw William tomahawked and scalped as he lay on the field, his leg broken, calling for help.

But we'd seen William come back that very morning, we said. He was riding by in a great hurry, bragging of cracking rebel skulls. Nickus shrugged.

What of the Johnsons?

"Huh! They didn't run away!" John and Dan and Guy and the other gentlemen from Canada had fought well. They were safe too.

"And Farmer Herkimer?"

"Cut down. Though he lives, still. His leg was shattered. His horse shot from under him." Nickus grinned at the memory of it. I remembered the big white horse scratching itself against our rail fence, its tail like a plume.

General Herkimer's troops had carried him off the field on his saddle and set him under a tree, the elders said.

"On he went giving orders, drinking rum and smoking his pipe as if he was at home."

"And the blue-coats? How many of them died?"

"Upwards to four hundred scalps. More taken as prisoners."

"Four hundred! Four hundred!" Mother's voice fell to a whisper. "Who?"

Those who knew spoke out the names — Palmateer, Hogeboom, Adams, McKay, Kellock — our Johnstown neighbors, and many of the big boys from school. Lana and Betsy looked fainter and fainter. I thought of the three boys from Johnstown who came to visit my sisters and were turned away. Were they lying dead now, like the ones in the field in my dream?

Mother didn't look sad or fearful.

"Traitors!" she cried. "Traitors! Many of them our own tenants. William built their houses, bred their cattle, saved them from debtors' prison. Gave them everything they had. And this is their thanks."

She glared at the sky over her head. "I will remember their names."

● ● ●

Three days after the elders spoke to Mother, a runner came with a message. Mother called Betsy, who unfolded the scrip and scanned it.

Betsy's hand flew to her mouth. I strained to hear as she

said it out: "*Herkimer dead of wounds. They will come for you. Leave at once.*"

It was Mother that was blamed for so many deaths. I looked at her, waiting for her answer.

She shook her head. No. She would not go.

PART TWO
Canajoharie, Mohawk Valley
October, 1777

As the War for American Independence spread, many British sympathizers fled their homes and took refuge in Quebec. In an attempt to make Canada the fourteenth colony, the Americans pushed their campaign north. Montreal fell for a time, but the bitter winter finally defeated the American forces at Quebec City, and Canada was secured once again as a British base.

George Washington's Continental army was more successful in the south. In early 1776 the British gave up Boston. In June they lost Charleston. Triumphantly, the Thirteen Colonies declared their independence on July 4. The British responded by taking back the city of New York in August and Philadelphia the following year. Then Washington won major victories in New Jersey and Vermont.

The British decided to use the Mohawk Valley as part of a campaign to split the rebel forces. They descended from Canada, aided by loyalist troops and one thousand Iroquois determined to reclaim their valley. They fought the local Continental militia at the battle of Oriskany, "the bloodiest battle of the Revolution," on August 7, 1777. As neighbor killed neighbor, Dutchman killed Scot, and Oneida killed Mohawk, the valley became a dangerous place for anyone still loyal to the King.

"WAKE the house!"

Someone was yelling, pounding at the door. I hid my head under my pillow but the hammering and shouts got louder. A dog barked outside, setting off another and another till they sounded like a mad hunting pack.

"What's that?" Mary whimpered. Juba and Jenny were sitting straight up in bed, their heads silhouetted in the moonlight. Juba lifted Annie out of the trundle.

I raised up and listened harder. Footsteps crossed the hall below. I smelled burning grease from a lamp. It was Mother, going to the door.

All week I'd seen shadowy figures lurking among the trees after dusk. I'd caught the light on their gun barrels, and bits of rough laughter floated up to the sleeping-room window. Lana said it was all for show, just rum talking, and we weren't to pay any mind.

But now the door bar scraped and I could hear angry yelling. Then boots stomped across our parlor. They were inside!

I slipped from bed to the landing and looked down. Mother was in her day clothes, arms crossed, facing them. I counted six men.

"Is Captain Brant in the house?" one growled.

"My brother Joseph is not here, Jost Kellock. Good evening to you, Jelles Fonda." She called them by name, so she knew them. "Search the house, if you must." She looked into each face in turn. Some hung their heads.

I knew that look. You had to be brave to stare it down.

The men shuffled their boots and three of them headed for the stairs. I flew back from the landing and dove between the curtains of my bed. A moment later the boots were marching through the upper rooms. Their lanterns clanked in the doorway, throwing long shadows across the walls.

They went from bed to bed, thrusting aside the curtains. Annie and Susannah hid their heads in Juba's nightshift, wailing. Mary and Peggy lay without a sound.

I coiled, ready to launch myself kicking and tearing at their eyes.

They pulled wide the curtains and peered down on me, monsters in the flickering light. Their dog growled and snuffled under my bed.

I froze.

"No one here," somebody muttered. "'S only children."

The biggest, roughest-looking man snarled at us. "Ye bunch o' brats," he said, shaking his gun at me.

Jost Kellock. The one with broken teeth who yelled at Mother.

"Tell that fiend from hell Joseph Brant when we catch

him we'll hang him from the nearest tree! There's good men
dead 'cause o' him! And tell the harridan witch who's yer
mother to clear off now, or we'll string her up too!"

Susannah wailed harder, and Annie screamed so hard
she hiccuped.

Jenny rose on her haunches, scolding shrilly. "You've
frightened the babbies half to death!"

"It'll be more 'n half to death afore it's over, wench!" the
man threw back. He gave the chamber-pot so hard a kick
it landed in the corner and smashed against the wall.

Then their boots crashed away down the stairs and doors
slammed. I heard the bolt scrape again. There were lighter
footsteps, and Mother's voice spoke in the next room.

"Did they harm you, Betsy?"

"No, Mama."

"Lana, did they touch a hair of your head?"

"No, Mama."

Her moccasins brushed the floor in our room. "Tush,
Annie, Suky, Mary. It's over now. Those men have gone.
They won't return this night. Well done, Jenny, brave girl."
I felt her warmth as she bent over me, her hand on my
head. "All right, Georgie? Peggy?"

"Yes, Mama."

She went down the stairs, taking the lamp and leaving
us again in the dark.

"It was only folks we knew," Peggy whispered. "Just
trying to scare us." I pulled the quilts around my ears,
muffling my little sisters' weeping and the servants' cluck-
ing. Slowly they quieted around me. But a lump of a sob
stuck in my throat. My knees wouldn't stop quivering.

Peter and Joseph told me I must look after my family. Peter would have stopped those men. He wouldn't have let them in our house.

"Peter," I moaned, just a puff of sound in the cold air.

No answer. No voice, no hug, no familiar poke in the ribs.

Who was I talking to? Peter wasn't here, nor likely to be. He'd been gone for so long there was hardly anything left of him to hold on to. Only a sort of ghost.

•••

It was still dark when Mother roused us. "Hurry. First light, you'll go to Hawns' farm and wait for me there. Gitty Hawn has always been a good friend to the Mohawk."

I searched her face for fear, but it was calm. Her hair was new braided, her calico smooth, her shawl pinned neat with silver brooches. It was as if last night hadn't happened — except she was telling us we were leaving.

"It may be some while before we come back. Each take a change of your warmest clothes. Betsy and Lana can help you. There are other parcels you must carry. We have little time." She stopped and took Annie in her arms and cuddled her. "You may also take one item that is most precious to you, if it be small and light. Now, Jenny, Juba — help me pack up the bundles." The servants threw on their clothes and hurried after her.

"All along she said we wouldn't have to go." Peggy stamped around the room and flung open the lid of the traveling trunk so hard it cracked against the wall. "We left one home and then another, and now she says we're going again!"

"Would you rather stay and be burned in your bed?" Lana came hurrying in, a dark lantern in one hand and her skinny shoulders all gooseflesh above her shift.

"But, Lana, it was only dirty ragtags like Jelles Dibble and the Staring boys," said Peggy. "Just folks we know."

Lana rounded on her. "Yes, folks we know — with guns. That horrible Jost Kellock, he'd as soon set us on fire as look at us. Did you see his eyes? Like the devil's, they were."

That started Annie and Susannah crying afresh. Betsy sat them on the bed, calming them and combing out their hair. Lana sorted petticoats and jackets and shawls like mad, bundling them into quilts from the bed.

"What shall I do about this old mantle?" Peggy fretted. "It's too small and won't cover my gown properly."

"Take mine," Lana snapped. "Goodness sake, Peggy, don't fuss."

I reached for my breeches. In the glass I saw my hair standing up like crow feathers, and my face looked squashed. Mother said we would never go, never. But now the rebels had come right into our house, it was different.

Mother and Juba packed blanket rolls with our clothing, rolled money into napkins and told the girls to hide the good spoons in their pockets under their petticoats. I put some down my stockings. Betsy and Lana quick-stitched strings of silver trade crosses inside the sleeves of their gowns.

What should I take? I didn't have fancy keepsakes like my sisters. My knife was in my pocket, and I didn't have a gun. I took two books that were small — the first part of *Robinson Crusoe* that Father read to us, and the Mohawk prayer book that Joseph wrote.

What would Peter want? I went to get his fiddle from the banded trunk, wrapped the bow in music sheets and tied it all up in a deerskin bundle.

Mother called us together. "That's enough. It's near dawn. People will soon be about." She didn't want it known we'd gone, taking our treasures with us.

"You'll come for us soon, Mama? Before this night?" Betsy's face was set and stubborn.

"Soon," she promised. "Cato and Abram will protect me. We'll try to save the house from burning, if the villains come back. When you get to Gitty's, tell her to hide our things beneath the floor and keep watch."

We tied up the dogs so they wouldn't follow, and Mother waved us off across the stubbled fields. Geese honked above in the early light. Betsy and Lana led, bent under their packs. I followed with Peter's fiddle, leading the bay mare with more bundles. Then came Peg and Mary, and Juba and Jenny pulling Annie and Susannah by their hands. We slipped through the gate and turned east, hurrying in silence over the hard furrows. My moccasins slipped on the frosty ground. Betsy kept us to the hedge-line to stay out of sight.

It wasn't long before I saw Hawns' chimney in the distance. When Lana knocked, Gitty Hawn drew us in like she'd been waiting. Juba and Jenny hugged us goodbye and slipped away back home.

Inside, the fire was stoked up and the room was hot. My head swam with smells of salt pork and corn mush and hot cakes baking. We set our burdens down.

"Mama says you'll hide our valuables, Missus Hawn," Betsy said.

"That's in hand," nodded Gitty. She was a strange figure, hair chopped off like a Dutch boy's and arms like a man's, bare to the elbow. "Sit and warm yourselves," she said kindly. She began filling bowls from the pot on the fire.

We sat at the table and ate while her big son Ezra pried up the floorboards. Down went our silver and crystal, French lace, family portraits and Mother's accounting books. Peter's violin was last. I handed it down carefully to Ezra. Then he leapt out and hammered back the boards, pulling the bit of Turkey carpet back to cover it. Gitty dragged a chest over that and settled Annie on top with a lump of sap sugar.

By now the sun was well risen on a clear, warm day. But Gitty kept us away from the window. "If anyone comes, run to the summer kitchen and hide down the trap."

Betsy said we should keep busy. Lana and Peg took turns playing with Annie and doing the churning, and Betsy lessoned me and Mary and Susannah with Gitty's youngest. I sat as close by the window as I dared. I near fell asleep listening to the birds, the bells clanking around the necks of the cows.

Soon as night fell, Gitty sent us to bed on sacks in the summer kitchen.

It was pitch black when a knocking set us scrambling up. Betsy hissed, "Follow me!" She opened the trap and shoved us down quick. I was crammed by Peggy and Susannah, someone's elbow in my ribs. We held our breath as Gitty unbarred the door.

It was only Cato, come with news from Mother. Out we

clambered, gathering round him while he warmed the back of his breeches at the fire.

"We was on watch right through the night. Half-past one, we saw folks inside the gate. They was talkin' loud, and they had torches. They come to burn us. I thought my time was come." He shivered and rubbed his hands and held them to the coals. "But yer ma had us pass from room to room, carrying the lamps. We was to make it seem that many of us was home. We set up for hours, and in the end no one came. I been sent to see you children is all right."

There had been more doings that night, Cato said. Some had taken all the glass out of Joseph's windows. They made off with Granny's good black and gray horses and left an old nag in their place.

"Miss Molly says stay out of sight till she come, an' be ready to leave when she does."

"Leave for where, Cato?" I asked. But he didn't know.

Another long day passed and the sun was going down again when Gitty's dogs set up a barking. We dived again down the trap-door. This time it was Mother's voice we heard. The door lifted up and there she was, reaching down for Annie.

"We are going to our cousins at Onondaga," she said as we scurried up after her. "Hurry."

"What about Granny?" Lana asked.

"I have left her with friends. The journey is too long and hard for her."

Out in the yard I saw two men and horses loaded with packs. "Narawore and Esau will come as far as Osagatchie Creek. Canajoharie is no longer safe for us." Mother looked round, as if she were telling this to the walls, to the corn hanging from the rafters. She shook her head. "On my own land, in my own people's village. I would never have believed it could be so."

The men helped Mary and Susannah up on one horse between the bundles. Jenny and Annie rode on the other. We filed out the gate.

"God go with ye all, Molly," Gitty called after us.

Narawore pointed into the blackness. "We keep away from the river until we pick up the trail north. It is not a good time to travel. The woods are full of bears."

"They're fed and lazy," Mother said. "It's the Oneidas who have sharp claws now."

I heard rustlings in the bushes as we walked. Cato said the people who took Granny's horses had their faces painted black so they couldn't be seen. The dark around me seemed full of dangers.

Close by, there was a sudden flurry and a terrified squeak. I covered my mouth to keep from crying out.

"Only an owl after mice," Narawore murmured.

We followed the bobbing white feathers of our guides' scalplocks. Soon we were passing by the village, skirting Joseph's house and barn. All was in darkness. But in our own house I saw flickering light.

I pulled on Mother's sleeve and pointed. She bent down close to my ear. "I left the lamps burning, so folk would think we were still there."

I stumbled after her, staring back at the yellow squares of our windows. Though it was only a trick of the candle-flame, I thought I saw a shadow cross the panes. It might have been Juba shaking out a cloth, or Susannah tossing her ball. And at the edge of the window, a shape was hovering, like one of us — like me — staring out at our ghostselves slipping by in the dark.

Then we were past the palisades and the woods closed round us.

"How will Peter find us?" I asked Betsy.

"We'll send word."

And Mother said, "God willing, we'll be back home together by spring."

●●●

Two days out, we forded Ogasatchie Creek, muddy and swollen with rain. Esau and Narawore lifted my little sisters down from the horses and set our bundles on the ground.

"We go no farther," they said to Mother.

We must go on alone!

She didn't reproach them. Oneida parties were on the move, and two Mohawk warriors would invite trouble.

"Not even Oneida would dare to attack me with my children," she said.

Our guides rode back across the creek, leaving us — seven children, four servants and Mother — cold and dripping by our belongings. They disappeared from sight, swallowed up by the forest.

Mother drew her blanket tight and took a deep breath. "We have four hours of daylight. Wring out your clothes and put on what dry ones you can, and fill your water bags."

I asked how far we had yet to go. "No more than four

days," Mother said. "Perhaps less, if we encounter no trouble."

I took off my leggings and emptied the water out of my moccasins. When the heaps of our things had been tied in our packs, Mother lifted Annie onto Juba's back and led the way into the dark woods. The sun barely showed through the thick pines. I followed in silence, shivering, eyes on the narrow trail. Roots grabbed at my ankles.

Cato and Abram went ahead to watch for danger. When it was dark, we stopped and made a smoldering fire to cook corn porridge. I heard wolves howling and crashings that might have been bears. But we were worn out, and as soon as we broke a few hemlock boughs for shelters, we crawled in them and rolled in our blankets. Through the long cold night we huddled together to keep warm.

In the morning Mother wrapped our blisters in soft strips of deerskin. With a hasty breakfast of parched corn inside us, we set off again. Cato and Abram looked so tired under their loads that Mother sent me to take their place in front.

"You must be the man and look after the family," Peter had said. Now I was looking to all the womenfolk, as he and Joseph charged me.

"Watch for Oneidas and bears," Mother said. There might be panthers in the woods too. At least it was too cold for rattlesnakes.

All at once I heard footsteps behind me. My heart stopped, but when I turned, it was only Peggy puffing up the trail.

"Slow down!" she called out. "You're too far ahead. Mary and Susannah can't keep up."

Her face was damp and smeared with dirt and her red hair was matted. I stopped and listened to her pant for breath until Cato came into sight on the path, with Lana and Mary following.

"There they are," I pointed. "I'll go on now."

"Mother told me to stay with you," Peggy insisted.

Peter told *me* to keep watch, not her! I put my head down and walked on without speaking.

"I thought you might be lonely," she called. After that she stayed behind me and for once was silent. In a while, my angry feelings passed. I thought it might not be so bad having her for company, if she could keep up.

I showed her how to watch for signs that anyone else had passed. The fallen leaves covered tracks of people passing by, if there were any, but we remarked some deer tracks and bear and raccoon scat. I showed her how to be sure we were on the right trail by sun and shadow and the way plants grew, like Peter taught me.

I walked lightly, straining for sounds of scouts or dogs — or noisy rebels. My ears were keen, but Peg's eyes were sharp. On the fifth day out she grabbed my arm and pointed down the valley below.

"Something's moving!"

I saw it too and signaled to Mother. Without a word everyone turned off the trail and slipped down a gully. Peg and I ran after them, trying to scatter leaves on our tracks. Hopeless! A dozen of us could not pass without a trace. Mother led us into a blackberry thicket and made us lie flat in the thorny tangle. Cato kept Peter's fowling gun ready in his arms.

I tried to quiet my rough breathing. Long minutes passed. I thought I heard voices, and then I was sure of it. They were coming closer. I made out words carried on the wind. "Corn," I heard, and "burning." Then the voices passed and there was silence.

Still we waited for a long time. At last Mother spoke. "Oneida. And women with them. Not a scouting party, for they would certain have seen our trail."

When she thought it safe to crawl out, I gaped at my sisters' faces, scratched and bloody from the blackberry canes. Juba and Jenny's skirts were in tatters and they had leaves in their hair. They looked terrified.

That night we cut branches and sheets of birch bark and made ourselves a proper sleeping shelter. Cato built up a small fire and made corn soup, so I went to bed a little warmer and better fed. But I had been asleep only a short time when I woke to a terrible roaring.

"Git! Git out of that!" I sat up to see Abram tearing across the clearing, waving a stick. He was bellowing at the top of his lungs, his shirt flapping around him. Something big and heavy crashed away from us through the woods.

A bear!

Poor Abram groaned and carried on. He'd been deep asleep with his head on the sack of corn, he said, when he was wakened by a nudge.

"I thought it were a coon after my corn, not that big furry devil!" His teeth chattered in the memory of it.

"Well chased, Abram!" said Mother. "He won't dare come back."

Abram hung the corn sack from a high tree limb and lay

back down under his blanket. I didn't tell him that bears could climb trees better than people.

•••

The ground was hard and white with frost on the sixth morning. Our water was full of ice slivers, though we'd kept the bags at our feet as we slept. At least it hadn't rained or snowed. Our corn was near gone. Mother wanted to save the last of it, so we turned over rocks to get crayfish and found late mushrooms under the leaves. I wasn't allowed to shoot lest the sound give us away, but I got three squirrels with my sling. Cato got two pigeons and a grouse. They were the food we had the last day, stumbling along the path on torn moccasins.

Peg and I still kept ahead, eyes out for danger. I was dead tired now, and my mind wandered. I heard Peg mumbling about honey apples and syrup cakes. I turned to tell her to keep her hungry dreams to herself.

Suddenly her eyes went wide at something ahead. Three hunters emerged around a rock face, walking straight toward us. We had no hope of hiding.

As we stood rooted in terror, the men raised their hands in greeting. "You are welcome, children of Degonwadonti." We were awaited, he said. Mother's relative, Mary Wabeso, was at the village only an hour away.

We stumbled on in great relief. As the light began to fail, I heard dogs and saw the dark domes of the long-houses rising in a clearing. The doors of the palisade opened and Mary Wabeso came out to welcome us, her braids swinging.

"You are safe with friends," she said, her arms open wide.

• • •

The Turtle longhouse was dim and smoky, but to me it seemed warm as heaven. The corn was so thick in the rafters I couldn't see the roof, and there were piles of soft beaver and rabbit blankets to lie on. Best of all was the kettle of samp and salt fish bubbling on the hearth.

When I went to fill my bowl a second time, Mary Wabeso put her hand over mine. "Slowly, boy. Slowly and only a little at first. There will be plenty more tomorrow. And the day after."

Children crept into the firelight, stretching out their hands to stroke my sisters' fair skin and play with Annie and Mary's curls. The sky through the smoke-hole darkened. Mother sat up talking by the fire, Betsy leaning against her shoulder. I sank down and slept.

In the night I woke stiff and sore, Lana's sharp elbow in my back. She was spelling in her sleep, the way she did when she was troubled. *The L-o-r-d is my shepherd, s-h-e-p-h-e-r-d ... Lie down in the green valley, g-r-e-e-n v-a-l-l-e-y.*

I needed to pee. Guided by the embers of the fire, I found the door flap and walked away from the longhouse. The moon shone on the humped shapes of more houses, smoke rising from each like peaceful breath.

We'd come so far, across rivers and gorges and mountains. Would we live here with our relatives? Was this to be our home?

How would Peter find us?

I WAS still wrapped tight in my blankets when the dogs began to bark. I heard shouts and a deep voice — a familiar one.

The door flap lifted and there stood a tall man in deer-skins. He called out, "Where's my family?"

"Thayendanegea!" Mother started up from the fireside, letting her blanket fall. It was Uncle Joseph, his head shaved for battle. She flew to him with a cry.

His arms went round her. "Praise be you're safe, sister!" He stepped to one side, his eyes dancing. The eagle feath-ers waved in his scalplock.

In the doorway behind him was a small figure squinting in the smoke. Granny Margaret!

She called us to her, chuckling at our surprise. She looked smaller and more bent than when we left, though it was scarcely a week. Mother had worried so about leaving her behind in Canajoharie.

"All of us are together," said Joseph.

"Except Peter," Mother and I said at the same time.

"Have you heard from my son?"

He shook his head. "The land routes are cut for us since Saratoga. The Americans hold all the roads between here and New York. But Philadelphia will fall to our side soon and we'll hear from Peter. Howe has ten thousand men there, and good navy support."

Joseph said our brother William was not dead at Oriskany after all, but safe at Niagara. But the rest of the news he and Granny brought was not as good. Our house was pillaged the day after we left Canajoharie. Our chests were turned out and things we buried in the garden dug up. The raiders found the Portuguese gold pieces and jars of silver and the rest of the trade brooches.

"Who was it?" Mother asked.

Granny Margaret sniffed loudly. "Oneida. They smell the changes. They wanted to burn the house as the British burned theirs."

Joseph took the bowl Mary Wabeso handed him and began to eat hungrily. "There were others too. Jost Kellock and Jake Picard led the plundering. The feathers from your beds were thick on the street. Then Farmer Dyggert took what was left for himself. All your Paris ballgowns will be jigging across the river at Fort Klock now, Molly. And your fine green dress, Lana — they say Dyggert's fat daughter is wearing it round the town."

"Splitting the seams," said Granny. "Couldn't pin it front nor back."

I saw Peggy blink back tears for the green dress. "Quilted China silk, it was. I thought it would come to me after Lana. To think of Caty Dyggert spoiling it!"

Mother said, "What about the Hawns? Were they harmed?"

"I hear Gitty kept the rabble off with a blunderbuss. But others say they were driven out. Canajoharie's only rebels now. The Mohawk have gone."

I thought of the treasures we'd left under Gitty's floor. Was Peter's violin safe?

Granny Margaret shook her gray braids angrily. "Blue-coats came across the river and took our corn. They ground it in our own mill."

"Their troops took the good houses for barracks and hospitals," Joseph said. "You did well to go when you did, Molly. It would have gone hard if you'd stayed a day longer. Albany jail, or worse."

"We're safe here."

He frowned. "Perhaps. The Oneida won't forget it was you who warned us at Oriskany. They're set on revenge. Your presence here is a provocation. John Butler wants you to come to Niagara."

Mother just laughed.

"It's best you think on this, Molly," said Joseph. "Colonel Butler has other bad news. His son Walter's been caught by Willett, the same rebel who led the charge out of Fort Stanwix. They've clapped Walter in irons and mean to hang him."

Betsy gasped. "Walter Butler! He was often at the Hall for balls."

"And so handsome," Lana said.

"And he well knew it. What good does it do him, now he's going to hang?" said Mother.

"Walter Butler was with Peter at Montreal, when he captured Ethan Allen," I said.

Mother turned in surprise. "You remember that?"

What did she think, that I was a baby? I remembered every word of the letters Peter wrote.

•••

Now Joseph was here, we all moved to the principal chief's house. It was made of boards like ours in Canajoharie, with glass windows and a fireplace. I liked the longhouse better, for it was more friendly, but Juba said a house with walls inside was more proper, instead of everyone together in each other's business.

Joseph had brought Mohawk braves with him for a council. Onondaga was still the great Council Place, even with all the troubles. The Council Fire had not been relit after the Oneida and Tuscarora went over to the rebels' side and broke the Covenant Chain. But the Seneca and Cayuga were coming from the West, so there were still four Nations united and pledged to peace with the King.

It was to be only a small meeting with no white folk, but there would still be many to shelter and to feed. Mary Wabeso said Mother was an important guest, so she needn't be concerned with the cooking. But my sisters wished to help, so she set them to clean and pound corn and make cakes and soup. The boys in the village asked me hunting, but I stuck to Uncle Joseph. He said now I was near ten, I should attend.

The meeting started quiet and solemn. Many faces were streaked with soot in mourning for fathers, sons and brothers lost at Oriskany. The warriors spoke scornfully of the

British, who hadn't even taken Fort Stanwix after so much blood was shed.

"They had no heart," said a Tuscarora with a fearsome scar on his face. "We lost our warriors because of men who ran away like rabbits."

There was much talk about the war and which side would be the stronger and whether the Nations should take up the hatchet or only watch and wait. I went every day with Joseph.

The third day all the women came too. My sisters and Mother and Granny and Mary Wabeso entered together. Mother had put on her best linen and her red blanket with black stripes for mourning. There were whisperings that she would speak.

The first to stand was a man known as Sayeyenguaraghta. He was the leading war chief of all the Nations. He raised his hands and everyone waited to see what he would say.

Peace or war?

Sayeyenguaraghta picked up a belt of purple wampum from the stone before the fire. "My brothers, the British beg us to take up the hatchet again against the rebels. But the Covenant Chain is weak. The King does not keep our links bright and strong. We have fought for those who will go to war only for their own houses. Who will fight for *our* houses? For *our* people? For *our* lands?"

He lifted the belt above his head.

"My brothers, I say to you it is time to bury the hatchet deep under the pine tree and keep peace with those who live among us. Let the white people fight their own wars. We will watch them fight, and send this belt to the victors."

When Sayeyenguaraghta finished late in the afternoon,

we saw Mother lean forward, as if she would speak. None of the other women had talked. Uncle Joseph looked across and caught her eye. Then he rose to his feet.

"My brothers, you have spoken truly of your injuries. But I tell you, do not put your faith in farmers who carry guns. They are not soldiers. They are not paid by the King. Brothers, the King has not betrayed us. His soldiers have fought for our people and they will reward our warriors. But the rebels have no money and want only our land. If we do not fight them, they will take it in the end."

He had scarcely done when Mother took his place.

"I speak as is my right as a clan mother," she began, as if daring any to raise their voices against her. No one said a word.

She looked around the great circle. "I have a long memory. I remember what my husband, the great Warraghiyagey, did on your behalf, to secure your rights against the greedy men who would now take our lands." All nodded and murmured, for no one had forgotten Father.

Mother turned on Sayeyenguaraghta, shaking her finger. "My brother, you so often promised to live and die a firm friend to the King of England. Now you sing another song."

Her eyes went from one face to the next around the council fire, and her voice rose. "You promised Warraghiyagey to keep the Covenant Chain bright. Is your word so weak it fades before your mourning clothes are worn out?"

No one replied, though some hung their heads. Mother's voice went on, filling the room to the shadows. She struck her heart with her fists.

"My brothers, I stand before you as one who has lost all

the great happiness I once enjoyed." Tears rolled down her cheeks in a stream. "Yet I remain faithful to my late friend, and to the King's cause. If I can do this, woman as I am, then who are you?"

All was silence as they watched her weep. I waited, not daring to breathe. Then, slowly, one elder rose to take her part. Then another. Some were weeping too.

"Degonwadonti, we remember our word to Warraghiyagey," one said. "We are shamed by your treatment at the hands of the Oneida." They would vigorously and speedily set right her injuries, they promised.

Even Sayeyenguaraghta changed his mind. "Let it be so. We will keep the chain, and our promise. I have spoken."

The tobacco was passed and the smoke rose. Joseph and Mother did not say another word, but from how they sat back and straightened their shoulders, I could see they'd won.

•••

In two more days the talking and the food ran out. Uncle Joseph readied himself to leave. We must come with him to Niagara, he urged Mother.

"Butler needs your help. So many are gathering there. So many hundreds burnt out of their homes, thousands chased from their lands. Fort Niagara is their refuge. They've nothing to do but make wild talk. John Butler's no fool. He knows one word from you goes further with them than any speech from him. Or from Guy Johnson, either."

Mother shook her head. "I will stay on here, Joseph. The children are still thin and worn from the trail."

The chief of the Onondaga spoke up. "Degonwadonti,

heed your brother. We are close to the Oneida here. Once your presence is known, it may tempt them to raids."

"So this is what is in your heart." Mother gazed at him coldly. "If you are so timid at offending the rebels, I will leave your house. My brother will take us to my relatives at Cayuga."

She was angry. She called the servants and we packed up. So we were off once again, this time taking Granny Margaret with us.

Joseph led us through the gates. Mary Wabeso and many from the village came out to bid us goodbye. We set off with some twenty others on the western trail. After a day's march Joseph and his party struck out north to the lake. They would make their way to Niagara by canoe. But they left us a guide, a gun to keep off bears, skin tents for shelter and a horse to carry them. Joseph said I should care for the horse, so I stroked his flanks to calm him, led him across the streams and found him dried grass to eat. I thought we should always have a horse if we were going to move so often.

Though it was November, the Dark Month, we were not so cold this time out. Our moccasins were mended and we had warm skin clothing that Mary Wabeso and our other relatives had given us. The going was not so rough and mountainous now. We sang as we walked, for this far west those we encountered on the trail were friends, not foes.

I was getting used to this strange new life. We would hear from Peter as soon as Philadelphia was won, and I'd write back and tell him about my adventures. I'd write about the trail and the bear and this horse. I'd named him Pinch, to remind me of my first pony, back so long ago when I was young.

~ 9 ~
NIAGARA

ON THE afternoon of the third day Granny called out from the horse's back, "Look ahead!"

In the distance were the Cayuga palisades. Peg and I were in front, but it had been a long day of marching and we were too tired to cheer. Then Peg stopped short and grabbed my arm.

"See there, George," she whispered "Something's wrong." Outside the gates a solemn group stood watching every slow step we took.

Mother came up beside us. "The Turtle clan expects us. But this is no proper welcome."

The people waited in silence. No children ran to greet us. No one smiled as we got closer or opened their arms to us like Mary Wabeso.

Finally an old one stepped forward. He was wearing the headpiece of the terihoga. Under the drooping feathers his face was painted with black bands.

"There is coughing sickness in the village, Degonwadonti," the chief said. "You would do well to walk on. We have lost many. My own daughter has died of it."

"I am sorry, Father." Mother bowed her head and turned to look at us huddled together. Our food was gone. We were thin and hollow-eyed and draggle-tailed. "But see my children. They cannot go farther. We must take our chances."

"So be it," he said, and waved his arm for us to follow.

We filed into the village to the meeting house, where we were out of the rain. There we sat on our bundles and women brought us hot broth and corn cakes. Mary and Susannah drank their bowls and put their heads on Betsy's lap and fell asleep. Finally Mother came back to say a house had been found for us where there had been no sickness. Some boys came to lead us to it.

We were warm, and there was food: corn soup and rabbit stew, beans, potatoes and roast pumpkin. But we were not allowed to wander about because of the sickness. So in the gray, rainy days that followed we played our usual games and did our lessons, and lay by the fire listening to the endless talk. Granny and Mother questioned each new traveler, trying to sort out facts and rumors about the war. Runners brought news daily to Mother, and letters came from Fort Niagara.

"Another from John Butler?" Mother asked, handing a sealed packet to Betsy to open. "Or is it Colonel Bolton who courts me? Butler says even the fort commander begs we join them. Which will this be, pleading or *commanding*?"

But the letter was neither from Colonel Bolton nor Colonel Butler. "It has Uncle Joseph's name," said Betsy, puzzled. "But it is in English. It is unlike him not to write to you in Mohawk, Mama." She read it slowly, trying to make out words smeared by rain leaking through the oil-cloth.

"*I again urge you with great Earnestness that your Presence here in Niagara would be of Inestimable Benefit to His Majesty's Cause, & I need only add Colonel Butler is of the Opinion that your Words and Exhortations would do Much to comfort and Sustain His Majesty's Indian Allys in their Time of Distress.*"

Betsy stopped and lifted her head, puzzled. "It doesn't sound like Joseph."

"Read on," said Mother.

"I cannot read the next part clear. I think it says Colonel Bolton offers to send a sloop to Oswego for us. *So you would not be inconvenienced by undertaking such a journey on Foot.*"

Mother was looking into the fire, her eyes narrowed. "The British have bid him write it."

She held out a bit longer. But it was the elders who finally gave her purpose for leaving. The British had called yet another council, up at great Fort Niagara itself, to "secure the Nations' support in the war." Many were going to see what promises the King's men would make. The Cayuga elders wished to go, if Mother would come with them.

"The British favor you highly, Degonwadonti. They would listen if you spoke our part. You would make the voice of Thayendanegea stronger, and look to our interests."

Would she be tempted? The army was up at Niagara. Maybe someone there would have news of Peter.

"After the council, if it is not in your mind to stay, you could return to us in spring," they cajoled. The reasonableness seemed to turn her heart.

"We will go. And I will see for myself."

● ● ●

We made up our bundles and were grateful for our gifts of fur mittens given us by the longhouse. It was December, Tsothohrha, the Month of Cold, and rain covered the trees in ice.

"I wish we could have gone in the ship Colonel Bolton offered," Peggy said. "It's most inconvenient to go by foot."

"Mother says if the elders are walking, we must walk, too."

"I'm sure I don't know why," she sniffed.

At least we were well provisioned. Besides Pinch, we had another horse so that Susannah and Annie could ride as well as Granny. We had company on the march, and no fear of Oneida ambush. Waiting for us at the end would be Joseph and Guy and other friends from the Valley.

Still, the trail was long and cold. The Cayuga braves grew impatient with our slowness and left us at the rear, women and babies straggling along, with only Cato and Abram and me to protect them. The food ran low. The little ones got quieter instead of complaining, which was worse. I gave Mary most of my corn to hide in her pocket, but the tie-string broke and she let it fall in the woods and was afraid to tell me.

Even with new mittens and mended moccasins, we got chilblains in our fingers and toes. Lana shrank to a thin reed and Peggy got an ugly sore on her lip. "I'm all in shambles, torn by brambles," she complained. "And this is my last decent petticoat. I've pieced the others so entirely there's nothing left to turn. How shall we appear to such society as is there, all bedraggled and disconsolate as we are?"

We were a sorry group when we came through to the clearing and got our first view of the fort. I was astounded at how many Nations were camped on the vast plain. Across the river in the mist I could see the cooking fires and camps of many more, thousands of tiny lights flickering in the dusk.

Colonel John Butler came out to greet us. He was a short stocky man, not much taller than Mother, with a red face and thin white hair and an Irish nose. Peggy whispered she could see nothing of handsome Walter in him. His words tumbled out so fast we could hardly understand. Luckily he had a trick of repeating himself over. He led us through the palisade, leaving our Cayuga relatives to set up their tents outside the gates.

"John, have you news of my son?" Mother asked at once.

"Yes, yes." Colonel Butler pressed her hand. "Howe succeeded in taking Philadelphia from the rebels with the help of Peter's regiment."

Mother's face lit up with joy.

"Only seven killed and five wounded on our side," he went on. "Rebel losses four hundred. I am certain Peter was not among the wounded."

"And how fares your son?"

"Not hung yet!" he answered, as if that was the best news possible. "But Willett swears they'll never trade him.

I hear he is quite ill, quite ill. I hold out hope, but — " He
stopped himself. "I hold out hope."

"God be merciful," said Mother.

Inside the ramparts, the old French stone fort rose up
three stories. Troops drilled on the square, and horses and
artillery and people milled about the grounds. Colonel
Butler motioned one of the men over.

"Come, come, Molly, let us make your family comfortable after your long journey. Here is a sergeant to direct
you to quarters." Then he left us, saying Colonel Bolton
would speak with her in the morning.

We followed the soldier down the log walkway outside
the barrack rooms. Mother linked arms with Granny.

"Poor Butler," she said. "He looks worn down with
worry. It does not look well for Walter. Though he's wily.
And he turned his luck before."

Soldiers stepped off into the mud or pressed against the
walls to let us pass. They stared at our little parade, and
called out greetings to Betsy and Lana, marching behind
Mother with their heads high.

The sergeant led us to a dim corner of the barracks,
offered wishes for our comfort and hastily left.

"Comfort, indeed!" said Mother, looking around. She
directed Cato to hang blankets for privacy. She told Juba
and Jenny where to set our things. At least there was a
smoldering fire, and we crowded by it.

Mother was organizing water for washing when Uncle
Joseph found us. He ducked beneath the blankets and
caught Granny and Mother up in his arms, hugging them
both.

"I heard they cleared a corner for you in this crush." He looked round at the rough walls. "Far from what you're used to, I know. But there's a roof over your heads and the safety of the fort. And food. More comfort than the souls sheltering round us have."

Mother fingered the blanket that separated us from the soldiers' families. She pointed to the girls huddled on camp cots.

"We had a better roof where we were. I would not have come had I known we would be treated like refugees. Look at our mother and my children, Joseph." She was winding up to a good speech. "I will not have them here cheek by jowl with all sorts. Common soldiers have already shown disrespect to Betsy and Lana. Tomorrow I shall speak with Colonel Bolton and demand the good lodgings he promised in his begging letters."

●●●

Tired as I was, I did not sleep easy. All night there was coughing and crying round us. Morning came dark and early, the soldiers roused before light and called on parade. After a hasty breakfast, Mother dressed in her widow's black. She pinned on many silver brooches and, taking Betsy and me with her, crossed the parade square to Colonel Bolton's quarters.

Colonel Bolton seemed a worried man. I thought he must have bad teeth from the way he sucked them and rubbed his jaw. His bones must have hurt too, for he got up slowly when we entered. He invited Mother to sit, but she was not inclined to.

"I will be plain, sir." She fixed him with her look. "My

brother Joseph tells me you promised him a house so he might send for his wife and children. But he has waited a year, his wife has died, and still there is no house. The welfare of his children causes him much concern. He cannot bring them here without lodgings. This is not well done."

She paused for breath and the colonel sputtered, but on she went. "I cannot be so patient as my brother. Many times you sent asking me to come, yet there is no proper place prepared for my family. How can I assure the warriors all will be done as the King's friends promise, when they see me treated so badly? Build the house you have promised, and my brother and I will share it."

We watched the colonel blink in surprise, as everyone did when Mother spoke her mind.

"Madam, we are in the midst of war!" Mother said nothing at all. After a space he cleared his throat. "But I will do my best for you in the spring. As I have promised."

Mother looked at him levelly. "We are agreed then. I have your word the house will be built in spring. I will act in your service and the service of the King. But it's growing colder each day. My poor mother is coughing. We have only the few clothes we came away with."

"Then you must go to the stores to provision yourselves," Bolton said at once. "We will charge the provisions to the Indian Department." He called out, "Sergeant McNabb!" and a large bearded soldier appeared. "McNabb here will see you get what you need." I saw relief in the colonel's face as we followed the big man out.

McNabb gave Mother his arm to cross the muddy

parade square. "So there's wee ones as well? Better wrap them up. None of you look to have enough flesh on your bones to keep off the chill. I've seen more meat on a butcher's knife." He threw open the door to the warehouse and nodded to the shelves.

"That's right," he said approvingly as Mother piled our arms with clothes and supplies. "Take what you can while there's aught for the taking."

That evening I had a clean warm shirt, thick woolen stockings, a blanket to wrap myself in, and a full stomach.

Next morning Mother was again up early, and she washed and dressed and marched us back to Colonel Bolton's office. I saw dismay cross the colonel's face when he raised his head from his papers and saw us in the doorway.

"Good morning, madam. I did not expect to meet with you again so soon." He spied the new red blanket round Mother's shoulders. "I trust you found sufficient for your needs? Is everything now satisfactory, Mrs. Brant?"

"I thank you. We are well provisioned for the moment."

"Then, what is it?"

"I have seen the state of your stores. How can you ask counsel from the Nations when there is so little in the way of food? Winter is upon us. I must be satisfied you mean to keep your word if you wish me to speak for the British."

The colonel blinked and rubbed his jaw. Mother went on.

"You've barely corn for a small village, not for such a gathering! Your bit of flour has weevils, as do the oats. You have rum in plenty, of course," she said bitterly. "*That* the

British can always supply. But where is your game? Where are the roots put by from your gardens? How can you feed so many people with so little?"

"Our provisions must come by boat all the way from England, ma'am. The navy is hard pressed to get through the French blockades."

Mother looked at him in amazement. "From England! There is rich land across the river!"

"That is Indian land, Mrs. Brant. The King has said we shall not encroach upon it, and Governor Haldimand himself has issued the order."

"It is good the King takes care to protect our land. But there are many thousands here," she said, her voice rising. "More than your soldiers must be fed. Our people are suffering. Many have died in your care! You cannot have planted. Where are your squash, your beans, your corn? Did you make no maple syrup this year?"

"Maple syrup! Madam, we are at war!" Colonel Bolton began to sputter at her hectoring and looked around for Sergeant McNabb.

Mother said he must set some of the soldiers to clearing ground before the snow, in readiness for spring planting.

He shook his head. "Indeed not! I do not have pioneers on this post for clearing land. I have sappers only. And those are well occupied with repairs to the fortifications, if we are to hold against the rebels."

Mother again did her trick of saying nothing, until he filled the silence himself.

"Though I see the wisdom of your plan," he admitted. "I myself spoke to your braves about planting, but they did nothing. Instead they wasted lead and powder firing at every wretched songbird."

"Braves do not garden," Mother said, turning on her heel. "You wasted your breath. For that you must ask the women."

• • •

Every day the land around the fort was more crowded with tents and lean-tos as the guests arrived for the conference. Newcomers camped together by clan and family, filling in the spaces between those already fled here from their burned-out towns.

The fort's meager stores were parceled out for hundreds of cooking fires. But there was not enough to fill all the kettles. The ground was bare, not a bush or a tree left, and everyone ranged farther and farther for fuel. I saw stick-thin figures huddling in the smoke. Coughing came from inside the lean-tos.

But all must be proper for a conference, no matter the deprivations. The day it began Colonel Bolton brought out some lieutenants and captains of the 34th, the 8th and the 84th, all in full dress, some with swords. I wondered what uniform Peter would be wearing now he was an officer. I searched for ensigns in the crowd but did not see any. Uncle Joseph led a company from the Indian Department, and our brother William from Canajoharie was in it. Joseph wore his captain's silver gorget from London and a beaded bandolier, a splendid shirt and a red coat. Colonel Butler drew up a company of rangers in leather helmets and green coats. Captain Tice, the tavern-keeper, was with them.

Peggy pointed out Guy Johnson, who we had not seen

since Polly died. He seemed shorter, and red faced and pinched about the mouth. Mother spoke to him, though the rest of us did not visit. I also saw folk from Johnstown who had taken refuge here. Old Yost Herkimer was one. I wondered if he knew how his brother died, shot off his white horse and his leg shattered.

The speeches were as usual, though there was less fire in them. No one was interested in war, only blankets and kettles.

An old chief in a ragged blanket stood and pointed his eagle fan at Guy.

"Brothers!" He doubled over with coughing and we waited till he stopped. "Brothers," he began again. "We have been driven out of our country by taking part in this quarrel. It was not in our mind to join your fight but we have done as you asked. Now our hunting is so lessened by war that we have fewer skins for trading, to those who ask ever more for their goods. This ruins us.

"We know you will give us powder and guns and knives and hatchets to fight for the King. But we also want shirts and blankets so we may live through the winter."

Mother listened to the speeches and rose to speak at the end. She put nothing of her harsh words to Colonel Bolton in her speech.

"It is the British who bring us guns and kettles and blankets," she reminded the people. "The rebels have no money. Our British brothers will feed and clothe us. Your old men and women and your wives and children will be taken care of, as they were when Warraghiyagey my husband saw to your needs. When we are strong, at the end of this winter, we will reclaim our lands with the help of the King."

It wasn't like the old conferences, where braves shouted and raised their tomahawks, but afterward Colonel Bolton came and said gruffly, "Well done, Molly. I shall write to Governor Haldimand to commend you to the King's favor for your loyalty."

"Then see I have not made myself a liar," she said back.

That night she talked with Joseph in the barracks. "If Bolton is indeed pleased with us, he may show his gratitude more freely. I'm housed no better than the wife of a common soldier of foot, with nowhere to consult with our people in privacy."

"I'll speak with him again," Joseph said. "He has promised us a proper house just outside the ramparts. But in the spring."

"He has promised me too. I have reminded Guy to tell the governor he has said it. But I will write to the governor myself, to see his word is kept."

She was planning another home. That meant we would not be going back to Cayuga.

I decided to make the best of it and settle in, until the next change should present itself.

~ 10 ~
THE PRISONER

"FATHER loved Christmas." Peggy warmed her backside at the fire and blew her nose on a rag. "And New Year. He would have arranged things, even here at the end of the earth. Feasting, and music, and games."

"Don't dwell on what's missing, Peg," said Lana. "We'll keep Christmas again, once war's done. We'll have to be satisfied this year with new moccasins, and dolls for the little ones."

"We had wonderful presents when Papa was alive," Peggy kept on wistfully. "Books, and scents from Philadelphia, and sugarplums and Chinese fans."

There was even a monkey with a tasseled cap and a jacket. Monkeys and sugarplums seemed faraway fancies now.

Some British families were planning a service for the Feast of the Nativity. Mother suggested Uncle Joseph might read the lesson in Mohawk. But the chaplain did not like the idea.

"Let the Indians hold their own services in the camps."

"Along with loyalty to the King goes loyalty to the King's religion," said Mother, repeating one of Father's phrases. "Many here are baptized. And they have forgone Midwinter festival this year because of our great hardship and sorrow. I am sure Sir William would not have spiritual comfort and the word of God denied us as well."

As usual Father's name worked changes. "I see your point, Mrs. Brant," the chaplain answered stiffly. "We must bring civilization to the wilderness. Please speak to Captain Brant on my behalf." He looked over at us. "Perhaps your children might wish to gather greenery for the chapel. To make the day more festive."

There was no green of any sort to be seen around the fort. Every bush and sapling had been burnt for fuel. But Peg, Lana and I were given leave to cross the river by canoe, if it was calm.

When we left the barracks next morning, the water was glassy, the ground white with frost. The guard let us out the south bastion gate, and we made our way through the camps and lean-tos, down the cliff to the docks.

The dock men grinned at us as we clambered down the path. My sisters were a bright sight in their red mantles and moccasins and leggings, half Indian, half ladies. A sailor stepped forward to help Peg, and she tossed her curls at him and pointed to the canoe she fancied. He made a little bow as he handed her a paddle.

I took the stern. The far shore looked near a mile off across the river, and we set to, our paddles dripping silver in the black water. My sisters' hair was soon webbed white with mist.

On the far side we lifted the canoe from the water and struck out up the hillside past the Indian camps. At the first ridge we turned and looked back across the river. It was a grand view — the fort rising up over the lake, the only bright thing the flag hanging at the roof peak.

The trees near shore had been cut for firewood, but up over several ridges we found scrawny pines and hemlock. I had a hatchet and an old knife, and I cut away with a will. Lana and Peg stuffed sacks with the scrubby boughs. A crow sat in one tall pine, mocking as we slashed. "Cawwk, cawkkkkk. Cawk cawkkkkk!"

"Look — it's old Butler, repeating everything he says!" We laughed and cawed back and felt much brighter.

Peg scuffed the ground with one foot.

"Wintergreen!" she called out. That brought Lana and me rushing. Peg was clearing a patch of glossy leaves with tiny red and white berries. I picked them straight into my mouth. It seemed a lifetime since I had sweets!

Peggy pushed me away. "Don't be piggy, George. I thought these would do for trimmings." She gathered what sprigs were left into her mantle. "And Mother can brew some up for Granny's cough."

By now the breeze was rising, so we loaded our sacks in the canoe and headed back. The sun came out, lighting up the fort and the raw shanties and tents crowded around it.

"Look there!" I cried. Northeast on the lake a ship was making its way into the harbor. "That'll be the last from Montreal before freeze-up." As it came closer I could see the men in the rigging, lowering the sails.

On that ship was the best Christmas gift we could have wished — a letter from Peter!

It was stained and dirty, passed through many hands and dispatch boxes in the two months since he wrote it. Mother's face softened as Betsy read it out.

Peter had indeed been at Philadelphia on Mud Island when the rebels surrendered. But Colonel Butler was wrong that he hadn't been hurt. *"They count me among the wounded. I was struck with a rough splinter in the Thigh & it has been slow to heal."*

Mother breathed in sharp. "Like his father."

Betsy read on: *"Philadelphia is sadly changed from four years past when I was here, but our old friends promise us Entertainments and parties. We are invited to a Ball at Whartons. Tho I cannot yet dance, I hope to be well enough to watch the ladies."*

"He's not changed," Betsy smiled.

"Though his writing has," Mother frowned. "Not so firm a hand."

"Perhaps he wrote in haste."

It was only a page, but we passed it back and forth. I read it over and over before it went into Mother's box with the others.

Next day there was more joy. Dan Claus had forwarded to us a package sent from London more than a year before. It was from Peter too, so we had presents from him as well as the letter!

For all the girls but Betsy there were pretty silver necklaces. They were tarnished with the sea journey, but my sisters put them on at once. But no gift for

Betsy? She was Peter's favorite. He would not leave her out.

Lana found the answer in the customs list. It said a pair of gold earrings was in the box, though we could not find them.

"Stolen," said Peg

"We'll write to ask that they be replaced," Mother promised, but Betsy looked downcast.

"They won't be the ones Peter chose."

At least Mother's present had not been thieved. It was a fancywork bracelet of cameos carved from pink coral, eight of them, and each a lady's face.

"If there had been time, I would have had them Engrav'd with all your Names," Peter's note said. *"As for the eighth Lady, Who shall she be? She might yet be a Sweetheart, but I have seen none in the world to Compare to my own Mother and Sisters."*

Lana smiled. "I see he doesn't remember our poor cousin Anne Elizabeth in Schenectady, who plagued us for tales of him."

My gift was a silver clasp-knife. I ran my finger over the pattern in the handle and flicked the sharp blade open and shut. I thought of my brother far across the ocean, doing the same as he chose it for me.

We trimmed the barracks chapel with our boughs and wintergreen. Very cheerful it looked and smelled too. The barracks hummed with busyness. The cooks made Christmas porridge for supper and baked bread above the usual allowance. Betsy and Lana and Peg were up early Christmas Day, turning hems and talking about a New Year's ball.

I left them to it and went out to watch the parade exercise. Some privates had put sprigs of green in their buttonholes and caps, and I picked up one from the ground for my coat. Along with some other barracks boys I fell in behind the line, and we followed the drill with make-believe muskets.

"Attention!"

"Poise your firelocks!"

"Cock your firelocks!"

"Present!"

"Fire!"

They didn't fire — that would be a waste of powder and ball — but went charging and ramming and turning about, closing ranks and fixing bayonets and advancing. And so did I, in proper order. It warmed me up, and I yelled at the bayonet charge the same as the soldiers.

Then Colonel Bolton had a parade review and after that a courts-martial. But it was Christmas Day, so there weren't floggings or hangings, just some who lost pay for being drunk. Then all the men had to put their kit out and show they hadn't sold it. If their coats were very worn, some got new. Old coats went to people lined up waiting for castoffs. I wished I'd got an old red coat, but our family wasn't so needy as some.

At chapel there were two services, one for the English and another for the principal folk of the Nations. Uncle Joseph read the gospel in Mohawk, and we sang hymns. I sat at the front with Mother and the chiefs. The rest of the day the sutlers' stores were packed with men buying special measures of tobacco and rum. The barracks rang with singing late in the afternoon.

New Year came next, with a grand ball in Navy Hall. Peg wanted to put her hair up, but Mother said no. She sat with the wives, keeping a sharp eye on the officers lined up to dance with Betsy and Lana in their made-over gowns. Peggy and Susannah and Mary were twirled about in turns. Annie tore up and down the floor on the arm of a drummer boy not much bigger than herself. I didn't dance, but I leaned against the wall, rubbing my new knife and humming the tunes — "King George the Third's Minuet," and "Gathering Peascods," and Peter's favorite, "The White Cockade."

Peggy spun by. "If Peter's at the Whartons, I'm sure he'll be dancing," she called out. Not if his thigh wound was still bad, I thought. He'd be standing by, listening, like me.

•••

Once the ice got hard, I went onto the river to watch the troops drill. Other times I went hunting with the boys from camp. Abram and Cato were glad of what game I got, sometimes a squirrel or a rabbit. One day we caught a sleepy porcupine, and the women showed us how to roll it in mud and bake it, then crack it open for the roast meat.

Winter was long and dreary, but March came at last. Colonel Bolton made good his word on our house. He had the timber cut and milled and dragged in by oxen. Every day we watched the walls rise. And as he promised, the Colonel sent rebel prisoners to help clear the fields for planting when the ground thawed.

One day I was coming back from hunting, four fine pigeons hanging from my belt, when one of the prisoners called out.

"Johnson!"

The other boys stopped in surprise. "He's hailing you."

The man limped toward me. When he got close, I saw he was missing an eye and part of his hand. His hair and beard were matted and filthy. I could smell him.

"Do you not know me, boy?"

I did know him, somehow. He tried to grab me and I fell back and stared.

"I know *you* for one of the mongrel part of your family! Curse every man Jack of them and their wenches too! Hundreds of half-breed Johnson bastards round the Valley. Deserve exterminating, every one." He spat on the ground by my feet.

A guard bellowed, "Fall back, fellow!"

"Boy," the prisoner roared, "I'm speaking of your pa, the great Sir Willie, and his dusky gals. No decent white woman would go with him."

The guard reached us. "Attend to your digging, wretch!" He thrust his bayonet at the man's ribs and motioned with his head I should run off. I stood fixed like a bird before a snake.

The prisoner thrust aside the bayonet. "Tell Miss Molly it's Jost Kellock sends his compliments," he snarled over his shoulder as he limped away.

That night I could scarcely eat or say a word.

"Are you ill?" asked Mother. I shook my head no but she put her hand under my chin and made me meet her eye. "Something's troubling you."

When I told her about Jost Kellock, she stormed out and across the compound. I hunched by the fire, shamed and anxious.

"She's not cross at you, George," said Lana. "You did nothing wrong."

Mother returned with Uncle Joseph. She was still angry.

"It was that brute, Kellock," she said. "The same who drove us from our house in Canajoharie. Bolton refuses to have him flogged. I told him I dreamt he gave me Kellock's head to kick around the fort!"

Joseph grinned.

"It's no matter for laughing, Joseph. George, you'll not go near the man again."

I didn't wish to! She said no more, but after a week, she called us together. Uncle Joseph was there too.

"Lana and Betsy have had their schooling in Schenectady, but George and Peggy were interrupted. Colonel Bolton has given them leave to go to Montreal as a favor to me. I have asked him to write to Governor Haldimand to arrange it. Soon as the ice breaks, he'll fix transport and lodging."

"Montreal? Betsy and Lana lesson us here!" I cried.

"As well as they can, but it's not proper schooling. Without learning, you're at the mercy of those who take our land and our cornfields and leave only promises. You must all learn to write on their papers and cipher their numbers. Your father sent Peter to school, and the rest of you must have the same."

Mary leaned on Mother's arm. "Us too, Mama?"

"When you are older. You are only eight and too young."

"Where will we live?" said Peggy, excited. "Will we board with John and Lady Mary? I hear they have a grand house in Montreal. Or with Dan and Nancy? That would be nice."

I hung my head. I was being sent away.

"Peter said I was to watch over you."

"So you have," said Uncle Joseph. "On the trail you were alert and resourceful. Your mother praised you. But I can guard the family now."

The room went quiet. I heard things in my head — the sound of Jost Kellock spitting, the sound of boots tramping.

"The night the men came," I said, hoarse. "He looked in my bed. He said we were only children! If I'd had my knife, I'd have done it. I'd have driven it into his black heart!"

All stared at me, amazed. I fled.

~ 11 ~

EXILE

THE wind was up. Our luggage had been stowed since
dawn, and by early morning the sailors were unfurling
the sails, which luffed and heaved in the freshening
breeze. The ropes creaked and the ship tugged at its moor-
ings like it was impatient to be under way.

Mother kissed Peggy and me in turn. "Apply yourselves. Make me proud of you." Though my sisters were
weeping, Mother's eyes were dry.

"We'll miss you, Peggy," said Betsy, hugging her one
last time. "Try to curb your temper. You're much prettier
when you're sweet."

"Courage, Georgie," Lana whispered and squeezed my
hand. They filed back across the gangplank.

"Bye, Georgie! Bye, Peg!" Mary waved over her shoulder.

As soon as they were back on the wharf, the prisoners
were marched aboard, a dozen captured rebels shipped to
Montreal for trading. One had his arm in a sling and a
patch over his blinded eye. His clothes were rags. I stared
at him in horror.

The rag-man whirled about on the gangplank. "Good-day to you, Mistress Johnson!" he called back to Mother. "A pleasure to see ye looking so well. And all your mewling brats too. May ye burn in hell, the lot of yez!"

He lifted both his arms in chains and shook them. A soldier shouted and prodded him with his musket. Jost Kellock — for it was he — spat in the water and shuffled forward. I trembled as the rest of the men marched by in chains and vanished below-decks.

"Cast off!" the mate cried. The sailors threw off the ropes to the wharf where Mother and our sisters stood. Peggy ran to the rail to wave.

But I did not wave. I could not look at Mother, who was sending me away on that same ship with the monster who cursed us. I did not want to go to school in Montreal. She was sending me as far from the action as she could, shipped off to be a silly scholar.

"I'm ten, old enough to carry a drum or be a fifer," I said to Peg. "Someone might have taken me on."

"Don't be silly, George." Peg kept on waving her handkerchief until the figures on the dock were specks. "You're not near as old as Peter when he joined up. Don't brood. It won't be so bad."

"It will."

"When I went away to school in Schenectady I expected to cry my eyes out with homesickness, but I was hardly sad at all."

"That wasn't the same. Betsy and Lana were with you. In Montreal I'll be at school with no one, not a friend to my name."

"Same as me. But I expect to make friends, and you must do the same," she said firmly. "And now I'm cold and going below."

She went to sit with Captain Andrews' wife and children in their cabin. I stayed on deck as we cleared the harbor, misery weighing on me like a stone. Sometimes the ship tacked near to shore, and sometimes I could see dark forests or tiny cabins in a clearing. Then we'd come about and the land would grow smaller and smaller till it disappeared under the waves. Nothing but sky and water — more than I'd seen in my life.

Captain Andrews appeared at the rail. "Not seasick, are you, boy?"

I shook my head, eyes cast down.

"It takes a day or two to get your sea legs. By then we'll be at Carleton Island. The rest of your way is up the river by bateau."

I raised my head in alarm. "Not with the prisoners, sir?"

"Not in the same boat, if that's what you mean." He peered into my face. "So Mrs. Brant's sending you to Montreal to make your way in the world?"

"Only to school."

"Aye, that's right. While this war's on, get your learning when you can."

I nodded and felt brighter. "Could I stand watch, sir?" I'd counted only six soldiers on board.

"We're safe enough. Nothing can touch this ship for speed." Then he seemed to reconsider. "But I'd be pleased to have you keep a sharp eye out for rebel sail. Mind you call out."

All I saw was birds. The wind kept up and next evening we reached Carleton Island and anchored off the harbor. When we woke, it was to the sight of cliffs rising above us in the morning mist. We were ferried to shore in small boats along with the other passengers and the troops. The prisoners came off after, and Peg and I walked as far away from them as we could. Neither of us wished to meet Jost Kellock again.

"Don't leave the dockside," Mrs. Andrews warned us. I could see wooden fortifications atop the cliff, ox-carts and laborers and soldiers going up and down the steep track. A fort was to be built there soon, to be named after Governor Haldimand — the same as was sending me to school. I scowled up at the palisades.

Mrs. Andrews called us back for tea, and soon we were saying farewell, handed into a bateau along with some soldiers' wives and their babes. There were four boats in our convoy, and when ours sailed near to the one with the prisoners aboard, I turned my back.

We mostly slept under canvas, but one night was too cold. We put in at a house and had hot bread and stew.

The rapids were high and fast and the boats flew along and sometimes leapt about alarmingly, making Peggy shriek while the boatmen laughed. Where the water was roughest, they steered us into the shallows close by the bank. There were portages aplenty, and we got out and scrambled along the towpaths. The woods were thick with white flowers.

On the fourth day we saw the church spires of Montreal rising above the walls. Soon we moored and disembarked.

Dan and Nancy came down to fetch us at the docks. Dan was more gray and his hair not so thick, but Nancy looked the same as the day she left the Valley. She hugged and exclaimed over us.

"Three years! George, I would know you anywhere, big as you are. You're the spit of your Uncle Joseph. Peggy, I hardly recognize you, you've grown so ladylike."

Peg hid her arms behind her back. We were dirty and rumpled from our traveling. "The lace on my sleeves got rimed with tar, though I tried to keep it clean."

"We'll soon restore you."

Their house was only a short walk away. "All of Montreal is only a few thousand souls," Dan said. He gave a coin to the conducteur. "Send a wagon with their luggage."

"*Pas de besoin, m'sieur. C'est tout.*" He called over one of his men, who shouldered Peggy's trunk and stuck my box beneath his other arm. And off we went.

We spent a cheerful night with a good dinner, hot baths and clean sheets. Peg asked endless questions, and I hoped for news of Peter, but Dan said there was none.

All too soon it was morning, and Dan delivered me to school. Nancy had added a pair of Billy's shoes and two pairs of Billy's breeches and two shirts to my box. Peggy was to go later to Miss Pollett's. First she must visit the dressmaker to get school gowns made up.

"Perhaps a new bonnet and sleeves, and gloves too." She threw her arms about my neck and kissed me farewell. "Don't look so long-faced, Georgie. Nancy says we are to come to dinner on Sundays."

As we walked along, Dan pointed out the sights. I tried to attend, but I felt worry churning in my vitals.

"This is Sir John's house, though he's in England now." The shutters were all closed. We came next to Miss Pollett's. "Peggy's school and yours are but two streets apart."

We stopped to leave my box at my lodgings, hard by the school. The house was low with sloping eaves. A glum servant came to the door and announced us to Madame Recambier. She was a gray drooping creature, like her house. Dan gave her a purse for my keep and hurried us along the street to school.

He knocked at the door, and we waited. I looked at my face in the window glass, and a stranger looked back.

Son to Sir William Johnson, I told myself, to stir up my courage. *Second son to Molly Brant, nephew to the war chief Joseph Brant. I have farms and cows in the Valley.*

But the face in the window looking back was of no account. A thin-faced boy with eyes too black and hair too coarse, shivering in the wind. I knew no one here, and no one knew me nor likely cared to.

Too soon Dan's knock was answered. The door opened, and I stepped inside.

PART THREE
Montreal
March, 1781

CONVINCED *that a British victory would ensure the treaties and protect their lands, the Six Nations had given up their neutrality at Oriskany. All but the Oneida and the Tuscarora joined Joseph Brant to fight on the British side. To punish them, Washington sent General Sullivan on a scorched-earth operation, destroying native homes and farms from the Mohawk Valley to Lake Erie. In the following terrible winter thousands died, and the starving refugees sought shelter at the British Fort Niagara.*

The war expanded, Europe's major powers uniting with America against Britain, renewing old alliances. France joined the war in 1778, Spain in 1779 and the Netherlands in 1780. Much of the action moved to the south. British commander Lord Cornwallis destroyed an army in Camden, South Carolina, in 1780, but then suffered serious setbacks. On the northern frontier, the fighting continued in a series of raids and skirmishes, as loyalist forces from Canada swooped down to destroy the crops grown to feed Washington's troops.

SEEMS like this lesson won't never end. By the sunlight on the floor, we're still an hour from dinner. The schoolroom stinks of cold ashes and farting boys. My stomach rumbles.

Out through the wavy glass, I can see soldiers marching. Priests, Indians and traders, and ladies and servants — everyone is going about their business. It's only us stuck inside, pinched up on these hard benches while Schoolmaster Pullman mumbles on.

A tiny spider is dropping off the bench ahead, moving down slowly, slowly, spinning in the dimness. Will he land on my boot, or on the floor? I make a wager to help the time pass — two shillings for the boot, one for the floor.

Two years, near three, of Madame Recambier's thin soup and gray sheets, and Pullman's bullying. Boys and masters come and go, troops ship out all round us. Sir John's Royal Yorkers parade in the streets, and nearly everybody's father or uncle is in one regiment or another. But I'm allowed no part of it, shut up tight in school like a prisoner. And for all I write to my mother and sisters and plague Dan Claus for news, never a word from Peter.

Could he be held by the rebels, like Walter Butler? Pray God he isn't lying in some rebel hold and suffering. But Walter got away, and so could Peter. More likely he's south where the battles are. In New York, or Jersey, maybe off the coast. The lines are cut, but one day soon a letter will get through. I know it.

My spider's stopped spinning, stuck on his thread. It's like time's stopped still. If I'd known what was coming, I'd have dived off the boat that brought me here. I've written over and over to Mother to send for me. When she last came to visit, I begged to go back with her to Carleton Island. Fort Haldimand's full up with troops, they say, ready to leave for the Valley whenever they're needed. There's two full companies of John's Royal Yorkers there, and the second battalion of the 84th and Rangers too. One of them would take me, sure.

I'm old enough now. Last week I turned thirteen. I could pass for fourteen, fifteen even, if it's size that matters. These days they take what they get, I hear — young, old, deaf, wall-eyed and peg-legged. But unless I do something, the war'll be over before I get my chance.

Some boys have got away. James Byrne ran off last year to be a drummer. Scrawny Enos Newbery went too, slipped down to the docks and got passage up the river. He swore he'd join the Rangers and avenge his father who was hung for a spy by Willett — the same villain that tried to hang Walter Butler.

I take out the clasp knife Peter gave me and trim my

quill and pare my nails, the ones that aren't bitten to the nub. No matter, you don't need nails to load a musket. A rifle would be best, but I'd never be lucky enough to get one, and all the Brown Besses go to officers. I'd get some beat-up fowler, or a long land musket with an old wooden rammer. Can't fire at fifteen counts with those, more like thirty.

I go through the drill in my mind. You got to remember the manual, so you do it by rote in the heat of battle.

"Handle your cartridge!"

"Prime! Shut your pans!"

"Draw your rammer!"

I'm off in a dream, my hands twitching, when Pullman pulls his little leather *Rider's Almanack* from his pocket. "'Twas a keepsake off a friend who went down in a ship off the Antiguas," he often tells us. The *Almanack* is all Pullman has to remember him. (As if we cared, sniggers Young behind his hand.)

Each day we write out lists from it. We've learnt the birthdays of the King and the Family Royal, and we're working through Observations on the Months. We're up to August, though what good that advice does in March is hard to tell.

"Gather seeds near the Full of the Moon," Master Pullman intones. We write that out. "Use moderate diet ... Forbear to sleep presently after meat ...Take heed of sudden cold after heat."

"*ACHOO!*" McDonell sneezes so loud another boy falls off the bench.

"McDonell!" Master Pullman thunders.

"Sir!" McDonell lurches to his feet. Was the sneeze real or manufactured? McDonell's eyes are as red as his hair and he's shivering too, so it must be ague. Master Pullman must agree, for he only frowns and tells him to wipe his nose. "And not on your sleeve, bumpkin." So McDonell uses his hand and runs it along the black streak on his breeches, made from other nose-drips all winter.

"Beware of Physick and blood-letting in the dog days, if the air be hot," Pullman drones.

Dr. Dease bled Father when he had fits. It was summer then. Was it dog days? Was that why Father died? I remember Juba with the bleeding bowl, dark drips running down the sides under the towel.

Recitation's next. I hate it. I prefer sums and ciphering, I've a talent for them. When I was young, Mother let me teach sums to my sisters at Niagara. We told off the times tables wrapped in blankets on the barracks cots.

Here's a ciphering problem: how old is Peter now? It's six years since he left the Valley. Near sixteen he was then, a hero in battle before the year was out. So now he's twenty-one, a grown man.

He'll see I've grown too. There's hair coming under my arms and on my belly, and I'm bursting out of my clothes. My breeches are short, my shirt's tight and my coat's threadbare. Not that I'll get any new ones soon. With six sisters to dress decent, it's only Billy Claus's castoffs for me. And even that's stopped, now he's joined the Royal Yorkers.

"*The 100 Rules of Civility and Decent Behaviour in Company and Conversation*," Pullman says, starting us off on the reciting. We do the rules over every day. "Begin where we left off Saturday. Christian Locke, number 48."

"Put not your meat to your mouth with your knife, nor spit the stones of any fruit pie on a dish..." Christian's reedy voice trails off.

How long has it been since I saw a fruit pie? My stomach rumbles so loud McDonell snickers. Locke hesitates and loses the rest of the maxim.

"Nor cast anything under the table," prompts the master, finishing the rule himself. But he won't take a switch to Locke, whose father is a captain in the regulars.

The sunlight has moved across the floor, and now it's wiping the bench-top. Two rows more before it comes my turn. I watch the soldiers out the window passing up and down the street — red coats, green coats, buckskins, blankets.

"Lamb, number 49. When speaking of God or his attributes..."

"Let it be seriously and with reverence," Lamb answers promptly. "Honor and obey your natural parents although they be poor." Lamb's parents are poor, unlike Locke's. He's here a year and then must leave to give his brother a turn. He could have my place for the asking.

Our bench now. My throat goes dry. Mustn't make a mistake and give the others cause to laugh. They never do it loud enough to get a stick across their backsides, but some do snigger. They call me Injun George, or stupid Injun, just loud enough so Pullman can't hear. I'm not stupid. I've had more schooling than most here, truth to tell. But it's hard to take the ragging all the same.

"Johnson!"

"Wake up, Johnson!" someone's hissing.

"George Johnson!" thunders Pullman. "Civility and deportment, number 57."

McDonell punches me out of my dream and I lurch to my feet, blinking. "Sir!" What number? Where are we?

"Hats," hisses McDonell between clenched teeth.

Rule 57? Oh, heaven, they've moved ahead by eight! I stand. "When, um, pulling off your hat to persons of distinction, bow ... bow, and..." My mind is empty as the wind.

My eyes turn to the window, desperate for inspiration. A flash of scarlet — a soldier strides across the street. My heart leaps. I know that walk, the swing of the arms, the set of the head.

It's Peter! It's my brother, come at last, in a red coat with an officer's sword! I take a step out of my seat toward the window.

"Return to your place, sir," roars Pullman. The boys swivel round, mouths agape. I'm at the window calling Peter's name when the switch comes down on my shoulders. The master slashes again and again but I hardly feel the blows. My hands beat against the glass and I cry, "Peter, Peter!"

But the scarlet coat strides on and disappears around the bend of the road.

● ● ●

In the privy I sit and nurse my swollen palms. Six more stripes on each hand from Pullman's switch — battle honors. The welts on my back sting too. It can't have been Peter I saw. If Peter was here, he'd have come for me.

"Sleeping again, Johnson?" McDonell sticks his head around the door. "Pullman don't take it kindly when you snore." He takes the seat beside me, but I pull up my breeches and leave.

Outside, the new boy's lounging against the wall. He's Francis Redding, a big boy with a bony freckled face. He came up from Long Island on the first boat since the ice went out of the river.

"Bad luck, Johnson."

He hasn't spoke before, but I've been watching him. I saw he stuck up for Locke against the Scots bullies, and no one roughed him back for it.

"What happened? You seen a ghost?"

"Thought I saw someone."

"I could see that. Someone you knew?"

I hesitate, then blurt it out. "My brother."

Richard Young leans around the tree trunk. "Ain't the first time," he sneers. "He thinks he sees him all the time and tries to bolt."

I say it louder. "My brother, an ensign in the 26th, at Philadelphia."

"The 26th? A regular regiment?" Redding looks surprised. "The commission must have cost a fortune."

"He didn't have to pay. The King gave him the commission." Redding looks at me with interest, so I add, "From his own hand."

"Never!" scoffs Young. "The King! Giving rank to an Injun? There ain't no Injuns higher than captain. Why would an Injun get rank?"

"For capturing Ethan Allen in '75 when he tried to take Montreal."

Redding whistles. "Your brother's Peter Johnson?"

"You know him?"

"Know *of* him. My uncle was at the fight. He talked of it all the time."

"Say, ain't Peter Johnson white?" asks Young.

"He's your half-brother," Redding speculates.

"No, my true brother. He's Indian, but our father's white."

Redding and Young look at me in expectation. "Go on about your brother," Redding prompts.

I know the battle by heart. I tell the whole story, about Peter joining the Rangers, and the rebel attack on Montreal, and how Walter Butler shot his pistol and missed, and Colonel Allen surrendered to Peter.

A little crowd gathers. They hoot when I describe the Seneca and his tomahawk, and Allen swinging Peter round and round.

Redding glares them down. "How did it come out?"

"An Irish sergeant came up with his bayonet and chased off the Seneca, and clapped Allen in irons. Peter sailed to London with him as prisoner. Then the King himself made Peter an ensign."

"Only ensign for that!" Redding shakes his head. "My uncle said he should have been made general."

"He was too young, only sixteen."

"Damn me, I'm fifteen!" Redding rips a switch from the willow tree and whacks it against his knee. "Still in a school with babies. Because my dear mother wishes to keep me from fighting."

"Mine as well," I say.

We all go quiet with our thoughts. The war is going on

without us. Montreal may be headquarters for our troops, but what good is that to us, trapped in school? Last year Sir John and Joseph took the Royal Greens down to the Valley to burn rebel crops and starve General Washington out. It was a great victory. They trounced the rebels up and down the Mohawk.

There'll surely be a raid this year, to finish the campaign. I ache to be on it.

"I'm going," says Francis Redding suddenly. I don't need to ask where. It's like he's read my thoughts.

"How?" asks Young eagerly.

Redding just shakes his head. "I've made plans," is all he says.

~ 13 ~

ESCAPE

REDDING waits for me now when the other boys rush from the schoolroom. He's boiling with questions about Sir John and Uncle Joseph and what I know of the Rangers and the regiments. I tell him what I can and what I guess, and we try to piece together what we've heard. Twice I've walked with him and McDonell between supper and last prayers. The three of us hang about the laneways before curfew, listening for gossip about postings or shipping or signs of troops on the move.

We make our plans, figuring how to leave. Peter said to hold fast till he returned, but he didn't tell me to stop here, moldering away in a prison of books. If Redding's got a plan of going, I'll find it out. And I'll go too.

I decide to go early to school and speak with him. I leave the others at their porridge and soapy tea and slip out to the street. The schoolyard's empty and the wind cuts through to my skin. I shiver there for a while, then lift the schoolroom latch. If Pullman finds me inside before the bell, there'll be more discord, but at least I'll be warmer.

Not much so. They only light the stove to take off the chill and leave it to burn out. Catch them wasting heat on us! The window pane is still frosted over. I stop and scratch a hole in the ice to peer out. No sign of Francis yet, nor anyone else.

I keep scratching away with my fingernail on the frosty glass. I draw a big square around my peephole. Then two smaller squares, one each side. I put triangles on those, and jutting chimneys on top. My drawing's a house. I've scratched out Johnson Hall, with the blockhouses Father built against the French.

I step back and examine this picture, then add the big front door and steps. Another triangle to cap the entrance. How many panes in the upstairs windows? I put those in too. I was only six, but I remember.

"What are you doing here, boy?"

My finger slips. Master Pullman!

No, it's a new master, the young one. Can't remember his name.

"Nothing, sir!" I drop my hand to my side. Make my face blank.

"And what is this? Ahhh, in want of a slate, you have used the one at hand." He peers forward to look at the lines in the frost. "A dwelling ... a fine one! Where have you seen such a house, eh? I do not think there is one so large as this in Montreal."

I will not tell you. I stand silent, gazing over his black-gowned shoulder.

He's taking in my tight clothes, old boots, straight hair. My face still brown, even after this long Quebec winter.

"Well, boy? Did you see this house when you left your village?"

"I lived there," I say stiffly. "It was my home."

He looks at me over his spectacles. "And what is your name?"

"George Johnson, sir."

He stares at me harder. "Now I remember! The old baronet's half-breed. You speak English passably well, boy. *Connais-tu le francais?*"

"*Oui, monsieur, un peu.*"

"Other languages?"

"Mohawk. Seneca. Some Cayuga, Onondaga, Oneida."

He jerks his head at that and his wig slips to the right. "You will not speak such here!"

"No, sir, not here, sir." I concentrate on his floating horsehair curls.

"Where did you live on that grand estate? Did you live in a wigwam, boy?"

"I lived in the house, in Johnson Hall, sir. With my mother, Molly Brant, and our father, Sir William Johnson."

He's nodding his head rapidly, making his wig twitch up and down. I watch the idea of living in the Hall make its way around his brain. "The great Hall. I have heard of it. Built after he beat the Frenchies at Lake George in '55. Saved us on several counts, old Johnson did! Took Niagara back for our side, eh?"

It seems he's talking to himself, or to the ceiling. "Gone these seven years now. Pity. We could use his help in these times!" He looks at me direct. "I know you now. You're the ward of Colonel Claus, Mrs. Brant's boy. Here on the

Governor's scrip. But then are you not Brant? George Johnson, you say?"

That is my name. I told you.

Suddenly, his tone is jolly. "Quite a family, I think! There are girls too, yes? Sisters of yours. At Miss Pollett's academy." He nods his head. "They're quite likely, I understand!"

Yes, very likely. My sisters are pretty, and clever. The young officers at Fort Haldimand all come courting Betsy and Lana. But I will not tell him that.

He's bobbing his head like a bird. I wait for further questions, another challenge. Then, to my relief, I hear voices and the noise of running boots. I look over his shoulder to the door beyond, and suddenly realize I'm looking down. The schoolmaster is a short man, and I am tall as he — even taller.

The room fills with boys, all talking together in English and Scotch and French. The master turns and strides to his desk.

"What's this? Boys! You are behind time!" He's striking the desk with his stick and flapping his other arm at the boys arranging themselves on the benches. He pays me no more attention, so I can leave the window and squeeze into my place. My drawing is fading away, the hen tracks melting, the peephole spreading in the center.

But where's Francis? I don't see him. His place is empty. Could he be ill?

Beside me, McDonell's scribbling on his slate. He slides it over to me.

REDDINGS GONE TO BE A SODJER, HE SAYS TO TELL YOU FAREWELL.

I stare in dismay at the empty place. Redding gone for a soldier!

McDonell's looking at me sidelong. He's taken back the slate, bending over it again.

YOUD DO THE SAME AN SO WOLD I SO DON'T BEGRUDGE HIM.

Francis has gone to be a soldier and left me here.

My head is still reeling when Master Pullman looms in the doorway and shouts my name.

"Johnson!" He catches me by the collar and pulls me to my feet.

"You are to see the headmaster." Without a word more he marches me off to Reverend de Lisle.

What have I done? Did someone know of our plans? Have they caught Redding?

But Reverend de Lisle puts aside his quill and paper when he sees me and speaks quite mild.

"Ah, Johnson. Your mother is coming to take you from school."

I gape, too amazed to answer.

"She'll be stopping with Colonel Claus and will collect you at your lodgings at the end of her visit. Madame Recambier has been informed."

He looks me up and down. "Well done, lad. We have not made a scholar of you, but you have worked with diligence. I am pleased with your good character. You will need both in what lies ahead." He reaches to shake my hand.

I find my tongue at last. "Thank you, sir!" I stammer as Master Pullman prods me to the door.

● ● ●

"*Allez! Allez! Espèce de gredin!*"

Carters shouting at their oxen in the street wake me. The noise drives away my dream of food and a warm kitchen and my sisters' chattering voices.

"*Allez-vous-en! Mieux vaut tard que jamais!*"

Something else is tugging me awake, something important. It comes in a rush. I'm going home!

I hear a commotion below. Mother's come for me. I daren't keep her waiting. Quick — stockings, breeches, shirt, my stock hung round my neck. I carry my boots down the stairs.

She's in the parlor with Juba and Cato. Madame Recambier has also dressed in haste, her lace sideways. She's gazing rapt at Mother, who wears a French bonnet and Father's jewels, with silver crosses pinned to her red jacket.

Juba smiles at me. Mother beckons for a kiss. How wonderful she smells, of perfume and woodsmoke. "Tell Madame to present Colonel Claus with her account for the Governor," she says in Mohawk, so I translate to French. Madame is bowing.

Cato and I head back upstairs to collect my box. His head bumps against the low doorframe, rousing the other boys. They sit up and stare sleepily at us.

Christian Locke blinks. "You goin' away, Johnson?" His bottom lip is bulging with an ugly cold sore and he looks alarmed.

"Yes." I forgive him all his sniveling and moaning. "My mother's come for me."

"Wisht mine had." His pinched face is stricken. Who's

going to save him from the bullies now, with Francis and me both gone?

Cato lifts my box. "This all, Master Georgie?"

I nod. Yes, all. Inside are two pairs of Billy Claus's breeches, a pair of Billy's boots, three shirts and beaded moccasins made by Lana. My Latin book, a French book, Mr. Defoe and Uncle Joseph's Mohawk prayerbook bound in leather. Peter's knife is in my pocket.

Back downstairs Madame is still gazing at Mother, who's smiling calmly back. We take our leave.

"*Adieu, Madame*," says Mother, to show she can.

"*Merci, Madame Recambier*," I say. And suddenly Madame lunges and takes me to her bony bosom! She bobs her head to Mother and we sweep into the street.

Seagulls wheel screeching in the clear air above us.

"You're tall, George, taller than me." Mother takes my arm and we set out along the dusty street. "Your sisters are all waiting on us at Dan's. We're to be on the boat by eight." Cato sets my box on his shoulder and we walk in the early-morning bustle to the Clauses, dodging the carts, the dogs, the bickering tradesmen and marching troops. The door is open, the hallway piled with boxes and bundles. I hear the voices and laughter of my sisters. And I smell bacon!

Everyone's talking at once. Dan tells the servants to take the dog cart and haul everything to the landing. We add my box to the pile. Most of the rest seem to be Peggy's. There she is, dancing round between the parlor and kitchen, chattering and managing to eat all the while. I take some bread and bacon to the corner. Mother's telling

Abram he must stay at the docks and watch our goods. I pass him a chop and a chunk of bread on the sly and he winks at me like old days.

A fuss has started in the front parlor. Nancy has her arms about my sister Annie and she's pleading with Mother. She wants us to leave Annie behind in Montreal.

"She reminds me of my own Catherine that we lost to the fever so long ago. I have no daughter left, Molly, and you have so many," she pleads. "The house will be less lonely. Please think on it, for her sake too."

"Annie is doing so well with her studies," says Dan, playing on Mother's weakness for schooling.

Mother gives in. Annie will stay on here and have a good home and plenty of school – and plenty of bacon.

Dan takes a paper from his coat. "I am preparing my report for the Governor," he says, holding it up to show Mother.

"Margaret, Mary, and Susannah have learned to read and write English sufficiently. George has greatly improved in his writing of English, and as to ciphering, with a little care and study he may acquire more of that Science than he has occasion for."

With care and study. Oh, no. He'll make me stay too!

"Why take the boy from school now, Molly?"

My heart sinks as I hear Dan commence his argument. "He's better here than on Carleton Island, where he'll be in danger of being recruited. You've given one son to the King's war. Let your second be a scholar."

Mother gives him a look that could curl coat-tails. "You say George will have more science than occasion for it?

Then I take it you mean he has enough for his present needs. No, thank you, Dan. He comes home with me."

Her tone permits no argument. I breathe again.

I'm going.

Betsy explains to Dan and Nancy that it's much nicer on Carleton Island than they might think. "There's a house built for Mother with room for us all. Proper beds and proper meals, even a bit of society."

I don't care much for society, but I know there's soldiers on the island. Finally I'll get my chance to make someone listen. I'll manage to convince *someone* I can be useful, for sure.

But I'll have Mother to manage first.

~ 14 ~
CARLETON ISLAND

OF COURSE it's Mother does the managing. We've no more docked at the island and started up the steep track to Fort Haldimand than she's giving me orders.

"You'll best put yourself to work, George. We all have much to do. You'll not be lazing about any longer."

Is that her idea of my life in school? I keep my silence and follow her up the path, carrying the boxes she wouldn't trust to the dockmen.

When she stops to catch her breath, I set down my load and look back on the harbor. On the flats below the bluff, men are swarming everywhere — scouts in buckskins, shipwrights building, carters loading and offloading. Nobody lazing about that I can see.

"Lana's kept the accounts, but she's needed for nursing. So we'll take Dan's report as right and put your ciphering to use. You'll take up her ledgering. And I have letters for the Governor that must be writ in a good hand."

She's getting the wind up, shaking her finger at me. "The King must be told how it stands with the Nations. He must hear it direct!" There's no need to answer. I see she plans on getting a good return on my schooling.

So it turns out. Hardly a day's passed and I'm hard at it, scratching away. After three long years, I'm free of school but not of schoolwork! But, blast me, it's April. My head swims with the green smells the window lets in and the sounds of folk coming and going. Inside it's as dark and smoky as the longhouse at Onondaga. There I'd be fishing. Here I'm stuck to a table doing sums.

My lucky sisters spend little enough time indoors. There's Jenny and Juba to do the housework, and plenty of hands for other tasks. Mother's collected Mohawk women to work in the garden. She sets Mary and Susannah to weeding and pulling off bugs, but they don't have any other chores as far as I can tell.

Peggy has learned quick to keep out of her way. She's at the hospital with Betsy and Lana, rolling bandages and dosing scurvy cases. I see her talking and laughing with the young officers, no different from when she was at school.

It's Betsy that's changed. She's eighteen, full grown, not so tall as Lana but more rounded. But she doesn't go over to the canteen with the other girls, who put on clean petticoats just to cross to the commissary where there's nothing to buy but tobacco and soap.

She keeps an eye on the harbor. When a ship comes from Niagara, she runs to see if there's a letter from Dr. Kerr. Till a month ago he was surgeon here at the island. Now he sends her letters with every boat. Betsy tells parts out to Mother but she doesn't let anyone else read them, not even Lana.

I sigh and suck my quill and tot up another column. It's so much like school I wouldn't be surprised to hear Master Pullman's voice behind me.

"Ho, Johnson!"

I jump. Someone ducks through the doorway. But it's not Pullman.

Francis Redding!

I'm so struck with amazement my arms hang limp. He grasps my hand and pumps it heartily. He's kitted out in uniform.

"Heard you was coming down," he grins. "My company was patrolling, so I couldn't come out to greet you with a proper pipes and drum. But you're welcome to Fort Haldimand, Johnson. If you don't mind mud and vermin, it's a grand place. Now, don't say you've forgot me so soon. You must have known I'd turn up again."

I point at his red tunic, his plaid over one shoulder. "The 84th." I'm amazed to see him a soldier.

He swells with pride. "Royal Highlander. I'll tell you it all if you come shooting in the morning. Veder and me got leave to go birding." He motions with his thumb and I see another boy out in the sunlight.

"I don't have a musket. Where are you going?"

"To the marsh at Grande Isle. Ducks are molting and can't fly."

Peggy and Lana turn up just then. Peggy smiles at Francis, but I guess she'd smile at any handsome soldier. Lana stares at Veder. "I believe you're Hans from Johnstown school!"

He beams from ear to ear. "No, miss, that's my older brother. I'm Jacob. All us Veders look alike."

"We got to get back to barracks," says Francis then. "But if you get a gun, we're setting out at first light." He wrings my hand again and goes off with a wave.

From the doorway I watch him out of sight. Francis, a soldier! What a turn-up!

I try to go back to figuring, but my heart isn't in it. I'm in a fever to ask Mother. She can't call hunting an idle occupation. The garrison stores are stretched from so many on the island.

When she comes, I blurt the news right off. She only looks at me, then crosses to the cupboard and takes out a long oilcloth bundle. Her face is hard to read.

I unwrap it. *Peter's musket.*

"Bring down what you can," she says. "We can't depend on supply lines. Most all the cattle they brought up on the raids last year went for salt beef, not breeding."

She's looking at the gun in my hands. "It needs cleaning."

I nod, trying to look grave and sensible. "I'll need oil. And shot and powder too."

"You'll have to speak to Tice for that. We're not home in the Valley now. There's rules must be observed."

Then I'm alone and can run my hand along the cool barrel. I finger the stock, its nicks and gouges. I lift the musket to my shoulder and sight along the barrel, feeling the weight.

So Captain Tice is here from Niagara. Just as I'm thinking this, he comes to the door, a brace of pheasants in his hand. I know him at once, though he looks worse for wear. A finger's missing from his grip, and he's limping a bit too, though he steps briskly inside.

"Done with schooling, I see." He looks at the gun in my hand. "Did they teach you to count rebel corpses up at Montreal? Can you add 'em up proper and make out a reckoning?"

Is he making fun of me?

"Mother says I must ask you for shot and powder, Captain," I stammer. "This was my brother Peter's hunting piece."

"I know it. You'll need a horn as well, and cartridge kit. Is it the Rangers you're joining?"

In comes Lana and hears the last part. "Mama won't have that, Captain Tice."

"Won't have it? A fine lad like Big George here?"

"He's just thirteen, sir. He's only going hunting."

He frowns. "Hunting, eh? I suppose you'll be sending me on my way, miss, now you have a marksman in the house."

Lana smiles and reaches for the birds. "Never, sir. We'd all be much leaner but for you. Here, George, take these to Juba to dress."

Captain Tice goes out before me, then sticks his head back in. "Come to the quartermaster's tonight, boy. I'll see you get your shot. Birds are good practice. Specially when they lie low in the water like rebel spies. And tell your mother it's high time to get you out of those schoolboy breeches. Time enough for schooling when we've done with this business."

Lana frowns once he's gone. "Don't think of it, Georgie. She'll send you away again before she'll let you go."

I snatch up the birds and leave her. *Soldier's kit. Tell*

your mother. The words go round in my head as I cross to the washhouse. Captain Tice was calling me out for a soldier.

Big George, he called me. When I went out the door just now, I had to duck my head like him.

Juba's by the washhouse taking linen from the lines. Mary and Susannah are playing peg-doll. Susannah holds her doll up, wrapped in scraps of lace and calico.

"Can I have some feathers, Georgie?" she calls out. "Can I have 'em for my doll's bonnet?"

"Ain't you too old for such foolishness?" Susannah's nine and Mary's near eleven. They're not babies any longer. But Juba gives me a sharp look, as if to say, *When did you get so mean?* My sisters' world is as topsy-turvy as mine, and playing dolls must make things seem as usual, like before.

I reach up to the hook where Juba's hung the birds and pull off the tail feathers, passing them to Susannah. But I keep back a fine long russet-tip for myself. I slip round the corner of the washhouse, squat in the dust and trim the shaft with care, stripping all but the top fletch.

A feather for my cap — my Ranger's cap, like Captain Tice's. Or a headband, like Uncle Joseph's Volunteers. Or a tartan cap, the 84th. Anything but a quill for ciphering.

"That's done now, Peter," I mutter in the dust. "I'm done with writing. I'm coming."

One day soon, a letter will come, I feel it in my bones. A letter, or Peter himself. And they'll tell him, "George is with his regiment."

That will be something, both of us doing the King's business, just as Father planned.

At first light I'm sitting on a rock by the door, Peter's musket across my knees, when Francis appears. "Found a gun, I see."

"It's my brother's. Don't know the range. Expect it's good enough for ducks."

Jacob Veder and two Seneca are waiting with canoes. Veder shakes my hand. He's near six feet and thin like a reed, the bones of his wrists sticking out his sleeves. His hair's so fine it slips from his queue and swings like corn silk around his face.

The Seneca are Blackwater and Two Skies. They take stern, and Blackwater pushes off into the mist. I set a good stroke and feel him match it. In no time we reach Grande Isle, rounding the rocky point and heading into the swamp.

No ducks in sight. We wait. Blackbirds sit on last year's cattails, and flycatchers dip in and out of the reeds. The frog chorus stills at our approach. Then Blackwater points to V-shaped ripples on the water.

I ship my paddle, pull the gun onto my lap, tip out shot and bite a paper of powder from Captain Tice's pouch. Blackwater steadies the canoe while I ram down shot and powder.

There! Three ducks break from the reeds, their wings beating loud. Francis and Jacob both fire at once. A duck spirals out of the sky and they paddle to it.

"Next lot are yours, Johnson," Francis calls. We glide forward, watching the reeds. In a few minutes a pair fly up and I take quick aim, as Peter taught me. The stock slams against my shoulder and my face stings from the flash. Both birds fall out of the air. The drake is dead, a mound of floating feathers. The other flaps and quacks, wounded. Blackwater scoops it from the water and wrings its neck.

He holds the ducks up and grins. "Two for one."

We head home with the bottoms of our canoes filled with birds. Blackwater and Two Skies take some, leaving me six strung on a length of willow. I should take them up the cliff, but Francis has a ration of bread and we walk along the rocks, sharing it out.

"Sorry I went off from school so sudden, Johnson," he says. "I would have sent word, but the fellow swore me to silence. I reckon he feared the whole school would bolt along with me. McDonell was bound he'd come."

"So was I. But how did you go?"

"Saved up my shillings and saw they got into the right pockets." He winks. "At midnight there's a fearful knocking at my lodgings, and the fellow says my father wants me to come at once. 'Course, my father's snug in New York. By dawn I'm poling up the river in canvas breeks and a toque. When we get here, I jump ship and enlist."

He gathers up stones and skips them across the waves. "So that's my story. Now, what's yours?" He looks at me sharp. "They say in barracks that dispatches come to your mother. From Captain Brant. And Colonel John Johnson."

"They may come, but I've not seen them."

"Heard you was writing the answers out for her."

"I've writ some. Mostly rations and stores. Blankets and such." They think I share my mother's secrets. "If I did see news, I'm not free to tell it."

"Ho, don't mean to ask you to," Francis says quickly. He sends another stone across the water, six, seven hops. "Only want to know if you've caught wind of the raid."

"We know something, Johnson," Jacob Veder confides, dropping his voice, though there's only gulls to hear. "John Servos turned over. He's come a spy for our side now. You mind him when we was in school?"

I create a shadowy figure in my head and nod.

"He was older than us, hung on when the rest of the Valley folk left, put out he'd turned rebel. Then he comes to the island in the spring as prisoner, caught by Colonel Johnson on the raid. He told Major Ross he never meant to be a rebel, but couldn't get away, he was watched so sharp. He made a good case or else Ross needed someone bad. He sent him right back to the Valley a month ago to spy."

"We hear fresh word came from him last week," says Francis. "And dispatches went off to Quebec. You know what that means."

What? What does it mean?

"A Valley raid!" he crows. He draws back his arm and flips his last stone across the water. It goes eight, ten skips, a dozen without stopping. "We'll burn the scoundrels out."

"Aye, and turn 'em out of the farms they stole off us." Jacob looks fierce.

"No quarter, no quarter, I say!" shouts Francis. He shakes his fist and starts to sing loudly.

"When the King enjoys his own again,
Then we'll turn those rebels out, an' tar their hides,
Then they'll all come a 'snivelling, sorry and a 'snivelling,
And we'll give them no quarter, no quarter, no sir!"

Then he charges Jacob, pushing him off the rock into the shallows. "No quarter!"

Jacob drops in the water on his backside. Then he's up again with a roar and splashes us both. "Quarter," Francis cries, dripping and laughing. "Truce!"

We head back. Mother will be waiting on me for more secretary chores. I'll do what she wants, tot up bolts of cloth and ax heads until my head spins.

But if there's a raid, I aim to be on it.

I BIDE my time, but there's no news. Nothing in the dispatches either. Then one cool night in August I hear a scratch at the door. Two Seneca come in, followed by a lone Mohawk. This one moves to the hearth and sinks to the floor. His moccasins are worn through.

Mother gets up from the table. She would usually ask the purpose of such an unannounced visit. Instead she calls out, "Juba, bring three bowls." She fills them herself from the kettle of corn soup simmering on the ashes. I watch as the Mohawk eats as if there's nothing in the world but the bowl in his hands. The Seneca take their soup into the shadows. No one speaks.

Still I wait. Finally the Mohawk puts down the bowl.

They've come with the spy, John Servos!

The Mohawk's name is Deyoenhegwenh. He says Oneida chased them to the river, but they slipped behind the scouting party and stole their canoes and made a clean escape. John Servos is this minute in quarters with Major Ross, the fort commander.

The Seneca say they'll sleep in the Indian camp, but Mother tells Deyoenhegwenh he can sleep on our floor. She'll see what else he has to tell her when he's rested.

In the morning he says rumors are rife that Washington plans another sweep, coming through the Valley and finishing up at Niagara.

"We must burn the route first," he says fiercely.

•••

"Some say we move in October," Francis tells me. "If you want to get on, Tice is your man."

I find the captain in the shade of the barracks, talking to two gray-beard Rangers struck off on sick leave. I wait and wait. They see I'm not going to go away, and Tice beckons me over.

"George Johnson, Molly Brant's boy," he says to the others. "Sir William's youngest."

"The only male cub at Miss Molly's den," grins the sergeant. I stiffen. What do they think I am? Some runt dog? He claps me on the shoulder. "I know who you are, young lad. Your brother was with us at St. John's. Not much older than you then, he was."

"He's with the 26th, sir. Last we heard, in Philadelphia."

He looks at me hard. "You've had word?"

"N-no, sir." I feel foolish. "His letters must have got lost, or ... the couriers have been intercepted."

They're not answering.

"We can only wait." I use Mother's words. "Wait till we hear."

The other ranger speaks up. "That's right, boy, that's all

there is to do. Waiting's what we do best." He spits into the dust, and the other two grunt agreement.

"The other side has their troops up now. Don't know what Washington'll do next. They're in the parlor, boy, and we're out in the drive shed, just doing the harness, just waitin' for their party."

"What about Captain Butler, sir?" I ask. "Is he planning another raid? Are we going down again to harry the rebels?"

The older ranger, the one with his foot wrapped in dirty cloth, takes his hand off the musket shaft he's using for a cane and shakes mine. "Sergeant Staats of Butler's Rangers, boy. How many rebels am I going to harry with a hoof that smells like a rotting cabbage? This other sorry sight is Ned Hayslip."

These are Butler's Rangers, the best striking force ever formed. If they're beaten and useless, what good will the rest of us be?

"They do say Colonel Butler's son, Walter, is itching to be travelin'," Sergeant Hayslip allows. "All's quiet from Niagara, but when it's too quiet you know they're plannin'."

It's time for my speech, the one I've had in my head for two years.

I swallow hard. "Captain Tice, I'm ready to fight. I'm old enough. I'm a good tracker, and a good shot, and I'm willing."

They stare at me for a moment, then roar with laughter.

I hang my head and turn away.

"Here, don't fall back, boy." Captain Tice calls. "We're only tickled to see you so keen. But we're not in any state, that's the curse of it. Two-thirds of us are off sick with the ague and the shakes, when we're not missin' parts of ourselves entirely. If we had enough able bodies, we'd be up at dawn and back down the Genesee like hounds on the scent."

Says Staats, the one with the bad foot, "There's blessed few left to be had. Scouts from Niagara says they've been all the way to Detroit looking for any fit to turn out."

"But if they're looking — " I hesitate. "Something must be up."

Sergeant Hayslip is pulling at his nose. "Yep. Walter Butler allus says best defence is attack. He won't sit and hoe beans forever, not while it's raiding season. I reckon the muster's coming by October."

Captain Tice is nodding. "But when we go, it'll be right stealthily. They say Willett's at Schenectady with two regiments and militia, near twelve hundred men."

"Willett!" growls Staats. "That infernal hog-grubbing lurcher that near did in Walter Butler." He motions tying up rope with his fists. "Wish't we could hang him up. That's bad news, Marinus Willett."

"Aye, he's the apple of Washington's eye," says Hayslip. "That means they're coming, they're coming across. They want all of Canada. They want the parlor *and* the barn *and* the outbuildings. And we're sitting in 'em."

"Captain Tice," I try again, my heart racing. "Take me on. I'm ready to go, sir. I'm ready to fight until I die."

This time he does not laugh, nor do the others. "I hear you, George. I'd expect no less from you." His voice is gruff. "Your father'd wish me to act for you. Like I did for

Peter. But this war's the worst kind. It's civil war. Tearin' apart families and friends and neighbors, and all the lives we built. If we don't take the Valley back, everything's lost. We'll be nothing but beggars in the wilderness."

He's looking me up and down. I stand straighter. "You're big, boy, and you're set. Don't know as you're old enough, but these days we take all comers. What does your mother say?"

Always Mother. "I have not yet spoke of it to her, sir. I wanted to know first if you'd take me on."

"Ah, that'll be the mountain, getting round your mother. She'll want to hold on to her last. Do you want me to ask her, then?"

Will she listen to him? It's my best chance. "Yes, sir, if you would."

I turn quick and leave the grounds, feeling their eyes on me. Something will come of it. Tice will make Mother see I'm no longer a boy. But I don't fool myself it will be easy.

A day goes by, then another. I'm so worked up I can't eat. I know Tice hasn't spoke to her yet. She's shown no sign nor said anything of it to me. For once her mind is on other things besides politics and war. Dr. Kerr has asked for Betsy's hand.

Mother says he's a kindly man and a respectable one. The wedding won't be till the war's done, but there's a ball arranged in their honor, taking all my sisters' attention. So when Captain Tice's knock comes at the door, the room is packed with girls sewing. Even Mother is beading a pair of deerskin leggings.

Tice stoops through the door and makes a bow. "An unexpected pleasure, to find such a bevy of beauties."

The girls giggle and Mother rises. "I would offer you tea but I've been without the makings of it as long as I can remember. Rum?"

"Thank you kindly, Molly. A tot wouldn't go amiss. War is no time for tea." He goes to the cupboard and pours it out himself. Then he sits on the bench and tips it down his throat.

"As good as I've served in my own tavern." He shakes his head and sighs.

"You'll have your tavern back, Captain," she consoles him. "They harry us on all fronts. But if we are firm and every man does his part, we'll push them back yet."

A shrewd look crosses his face. "If *every man* does his part, that's the truth. But there's few enough of those left. We're pulling them off sickbeds and sticking wooden legs on their stumps. Your warriors cough all night and have no more fat on their backs than a snake, but they fight when you urge them. A word from you, Molly, is worth those of all the chiefs together. His Majesty himself knows it."

Mother nods, accepting his praise. My heart lurches. I begin to see where this is heading.

He lowers his voice. "I'd have a private word." She nods, and motions at me and the girls to leave.

But he's holding up his hand to stay me. "In George's presence."

Her eyebrows lift. She gives a sign for the girls to go, and they leave, reluctantly. Peg makes a face at me.

Captain Tice leans across the table to Mother. "Knowing well there is none more loyal than you is why I've come to support your son, Molly. The raid to come must be a large one if we are to press our advantage. We need every fit man. George has asked me to put him forward for what company will take him. Do you have a wish as to which he serves in?"

Mother looks taken by surprise. "Why, none, I thank you, Captain Tice! George is a schoolboy, not a soldier."

"I'm done with schooling, Mother. You said so to Colonel Claus."

She turns on me with a fierce frown. "Quiet! I brought you home because I had need of you. Not to send you off as a raider."

I speak as firmly as I can, though my voice shakes. "I'm not a boy, Mother. I'm grown."

She changes to Mohawk and her speech-making voice. "This is my decision. You are not to join the soldiers. You will stay here and do as I have spoken."

"Peter would go."

"Peter!" she cries.

Captain Tice interrupts in English. "The boy is old enough, Degonwadonti. He's speaking his mind. You must hear him out."

"Must? Must!" She draws herself up, pulls her blanket tight around her. Captain Tice has gone too far.

"You must feel it so in your heart," he says.

The lines of Mother's frown cut more deeply around her mouth. I rush on to keep ahead of my terror.

"Peter was little older than me when he joined the Rangers. You were proud when you read his letter, Mother."

Tice speaks now in his clumsy Mohawk. "I'll watch out for the boy, Degonwadonti, you have my word. As a soldier, and as a friend. I will watch for him as a son. As William would have me do."

"William — " she begins angrily.

Tice heads her off. "William would have seen the state of things, as you do. Last year Joseph and John nearly crushed the rebels. If they rebuild their strength, we'll never go home. We need every man. We have too few as sound and true as George."

We wait for her next words. When they come, her voice is bitter and old. "It will be so. I will send my last son."

I let out my breath.

"But send him back, Gilbert Tice. Send him back! If ..." She pauses. "*If* my son Peter should not return, then I must keep George. Or all is lost to me."

"I will watch him front and back, Molly." Captain Tice shakes her hand and quickly takes his leave.

I try to follow him, but Mother stays me. Her face is hard as flint and her fingers clamp my wrist. "You should have come to me first, George. This was not well done."

"No, Mother." I hang my head. "But you would not have listened. You do not want me to go."

"That I do not. But it has come, and on the eve of Betsy's betrothal." She shakes her head. "Such foolish happiness." Her eyes fill, and I'm shocked. "Only promise me that you will do all with care. For our sake, and for your brother's. You must return, for his sake."

She turns her back on me. I stand, waiting. "Mother?"

"Go."

So I do. I go to find Francis and Jacob to tell them my news.

~ 16 ~
DOWN TO THE VALLEY

CAPTAIN Tice, true to his word, has found me a rank.
"I've put you up for a Scout, on the Indian Department
list. That way there'll be no troubles over age."

That way there will be no red coat neither. Nor new
boots, nor cocked hat, nor anything like what Jacob and
Francis have. Just an old green coat and someone else's
boots and gaiters.

But Peter started this way, in the Rangers, so I don't
complain. They issue me the coat and boots, and a haversack and a cartridge pouch and blanket from the stores.
The only thing I get new is a pair of buckskin breeches. I'm
wondering if I should ask Mother for Peter's gun when the
Captain brings in a long land musket, near tall as me.

Tice has me take the loyal oath in front of Major Ross.
He says he told Mother, but only Lana and Betsy and
Peggy come. Betsy says they're standing in for her, but I'm
not fooled.

I say the words after Captain Tice.

"I, George Johnson, voluntarily swear to bear Faith and

true Allegiance to His Majesty King George the Third; and defend to the utmost of my Power, His sacred Person, Crown and Government, against all Persons whatsoever."

To the utmost of my power.

With my life — that's what it means. I'm the King's man now.

I'm thinking about this when Captain Tice hands me a tomahawk. "Bayonets are infantry issue for sidearms, but a tomahawk's standard for Rangers. Thought you might like this one," he says gruffly. "It's Oneida. From Oriskany."

Oriskany — the battle that started all this.

"Report at dawn tomorrow," he says. "But don't move to barracks. Ye might as well bide at home so ye can do your mother's accounts of an evening."

And make peace with her, he might have said.

At least my sisters take an interest in my fortunes. Lana and Mary make me leggings and moccasins, though they say nothing of it to Mother. Peggy's found me a beaded bandolier with a few fur tags still attached.

"It's not as nice as Joseph's," she says, "but you can hang cartridges or your haversack from it. It'll look smart with your coat."

"Where'd you get it, Peggo?"

"I traded," is all she'll say. I try it on for size and fold it in my pouch with my knife. Every time I set out on our journeys I take less and less. I've got it down to a small bundle of myself.

I'm oiling my gun in the corner when Mother comes in. I rub harder and keep my head down.

"You've got a long-arm."

I look up quick and catch her eye. "No, French musket. It's all they had, this old piece."

"All they've got is boys too," she snaps.

"And men. We'll do the best we can. This time we'll beat them."

"This time! This time you'll stay with Tice. He promises you'll be scouting, not fighting, if he can help it. Leave the fighting to the men."

I don't answer. I know she's feared for me. But I have a plan to make it up to her. I'll get to Gitty's and find Peter's violin under the floorboards. I'll bring it back, all the way. I put myself to sleep nights thinking of that violin and Mother's face when she sees it. And of Peter, when he comes home, taking it up in his hands and asking, "How did this come here?"

"George fetched it," they'll say.

● ● ●

The raid's set for October. Major Ross is in command, with Walter Butler second, in charge of Butler's Rangers. Captain David Hill is leading forty warriors from Carleton Island. Captain Tice has gone down to Niagara to get a hundred more Indians and meet us at Oswego.

By the first week we're provisioned and waiting out a nor'easter. Ross says we can't leave till it passes and we've a proper headwind.

When our good wind comes, I say my goodbyes to Mother. A cold kiss and I'm out the door. My sisters come to the docks, and Betsy hands me a pouch of pounded corn.

"It's from her," she says, and hugs and kisses me. I put

it in my pack to keep it dry. Then Lana must kiss me too, but when I come to Peg, all I get is a sharp pinch.

"Peggy!" Betsy and Lana both scold at once.

"That's to remind him to keep safe, so we won't worry ourselves half to death," she says fiercely.

By noon we're sailing westward on the lake. The schooner *Horton* leads the way, pulling a string of canoes laden with supplies. We follow behind in the bateaux. We reach Fort Oswego by nightfall, but there's no sign yet of Captain Tice and Walter Butler.

The wind is strong off the lake, and it's a struggle to set up shelter inside the ramparts. We manage a smoky fire and down plenty of bread and tea and stew, post our pickets and crawl into the tents. We sleep head to foot, six to a tent. At least it keeps me warm.

The storm hits us square. It rains all night and all next day. The mess-rooms stink of wet wool and smoke. Francis and Jacob and I hunker in a corner, busying ourselves with our gear. I've got my cartridges done up — paper, powder and ball all rolled and tied. I borrow a file and sharpen my tomahawk. I tell them it's from Oriskany, and Jacob whistles. My powder horn is old and plain, but I plan to carve it when we're done: *George Johnson, HM Indian Dept, Valley Raid, 1781.*

My innards are stirred up with excitement. We've not been told where we're going or what we're doing. "In case we fall into enemy hands," says Francis. But I know we're heading to the Valley to burn the harvest.

"We'll starve 'em out," says Sergeant Hayslip, doing his best to razzle our spirits "We'll empty their bellies and shift 'em out of our homes." We've all got a stake in this raid, he says — Dutch and English, Mohawk or Seneca. Winning back our livings or fighting for our treaty lands, it's the same fight.

The wind swings about next morning, and by nightfall two hundred troops from Niagara are here. That makes us five hundred, all told — regulars, Rangers and Indians. Numbers are low, says Sergeant Hayslip. "It's a shame Joe Brant's in the western lands, hunting down Daniel Boone. But don't let on, mind. It don't hurt to let the rebels *think* he's along. I hear Valley folk use his name to scare wee ones now — 'Hush or Monster Brant'll come!'"

It's a funny thought, Uncle Joseph scaring babies.

We hear Sir John's sent companies of Royal Yorkers south from Montreal to Crown Point. The plan is to trick the rebels into thinking the raid is coming from the east alone.

"Crafty," says the sergeant. "Willett's holed up east in Schenectady. He'll have his back turned, and we can get in behind and out afore he knows we're there."

We all know Willett and Walter Butler have a score to settle.

"We could set Willett up neat as a rabbit," says Francis. "Scout him out from behind and set a snare. Grab him and bring *him* back in chains."

Sergeant Hayslip hears and cuffs Francis on the ear. "Young fool! You got yer orders. Don't be making any of yer own. We're not after him, we're after his feed bag. We empty the larder and give him the slip. We ought to manage it," he continues. "They say the Valley is naught but ghosts, 'cept those places as got crops in. We got to burn their barns before they fill the bellies of Washington's troops. If we starve 'em out, we can turn the end of this war."

•••

All down the Oswego it rains. We wrap ourselves in oilskin capes and huddle under canvas in the boats. I feel the damp through to my skin. In the tent at night I wake a dozen times to shift my head away from a leak. It's hard to move, packed in so.

We cross Oneida Lake and unload. They order us to sink the boats so the enemy won't find them. We fill them with rocks, haul them out from the bank and pull out the bungs. I strip to my breeches and load our boat up with stones, and Jacob strips even further. Everyone roars as he poles out a boat, white and bare as a plucked crane. He splashes back to shore, whooping at the cold water. We get to warm our backsides by the fire and climb back into our clothes steaming and well smoked.

The rain keeps falling, sometimes fine as mist, sometimes like God and his angels are emptying buckets on us. For days it rains, and we walk and walk. When I catch sight of the sun behind the clouds, I see we're heading south instead of turning east to the Mohawk River. We're stealing along Indian trails, staying out of sight so Willett won't hear we're coming till it's too late. The farther we get without his knowing, the better our chances of getting out alive.

Now and then things look familiar. Is this how we came when Mother led us out of the Valley? All I can remember is the endless climbing, and the roots that reached to grab my feet.

Some red and yellow leaves cling to the oaks and beeches, and there's fir and pine, so we've got cover. Scouts walk at front flank, but Captain Tice puts me well back, being untried. I keep an eye on Francis who's marching in middle ranks. He's a corporal now. I can see Jacob trudging away, and then our artillery and supply bringing up the rear, with the light company as guards. After come more Rangers, watching our backs.

The plan was to commandeer horses to pull our wagons and gun carriages, but the farms we pass are deserted. They've yoked men to the harnesses instead, and they're struggling through the ruts. One wagon sticks, and Francis takes up a side and yells to the men to put their shoulders to it. We break ranks and watch while they slosh around, slipping on the leaves and greasy mud.

Jacob comes up to join me.

"I ain't looking forward to our turn. What'll happen if the axles break, or the loads shift, or we get attacked and can't get our guns?" Jacob's a prime talker and babbles on, whatever comes into his head.

Often we talk about Walter Butler, who's marching near the front alongside Captain Ross. "They say he's fearless but canny. He knows the Valley like the back of his hand," says Jacob. "Pa says all the Butlers is proud. Without as much reason to be as some, like the Johnsons."

"Walter's a hero," I say. I take my brother's word for his character. "He fought side by side with Peter and Captain Tice."

If I get the chance, I'll ask Walter Butler if he's seen or heard tell of my brother. Walter gets around, they say, in and out of uniform. He might know if Peter's gone down to Virginny or the Carolinas to fight, or maybe back to England at the King's wish. He'll tell me, when he knows who I am. I'll bide my time and ask.

"Ho, what's happened?" Jacob says suddenly.

There's a commotion ahead. Everyone runs forward to gather around something, or someone — a fallen man. Men are shouting and the officers order us to shoulder arms. We're fumbling for cartridges when the order is as quickly canceled. It's a lieutenant named Dochstadder. The surgeon says it's not shot that felled him, but his heart gave out.

Nothing to do but bury him. The sappers dig a quick trench. They take his boots, coat and sword and wrap him in a blanket. Captain Ross pins the regimental badge to it before they cover the body with earth and stones. He reads a bit of service in haste as the digging goes on, and we say our amens and then wheel about. I don't glance back.

"An hour past he was marching with us, poor soul." Jacob's teeth are chattering from cold, and more. "He leaves a wife and babes, they say."

Our first dead man, and from our own ranks. I hope it's not an omen.

Later in the day our luck improves. We catch sight of half a dozen horses grazing in a rain-soaked field. The houses and barns nearby are empty.

"Must have been in an awful hurry, to leave their

horses," says Jacob. Some Seneca scouts soon round them
up and they're yoked to the gun carriages in place of the
men. There's enough to pull the wagons too.

We find a few bedraggled chickens in a barn and wring
their necks. "Wish we could roast 'em," says Jacob. But
they'll be boiled in the evening stew and shared about.
Jacob makes me stand guard by the barn door while he
looks for eggs, and finds a clutch hidden in a corner. We
suck them as we march and tuck the extra ones in our
pockets for later.

Farther on we pass a deserted Onondaga village. The
homes are burnt to their foundations, the neat rows of long-
houses just charred frames, blackened perches for crows.
The fields are trampled flat and there's nothing to salvage.
Is this the village where we sheltered when we fled
Canajoharie? I remember warm rabbit blankets in the
longhouse, and corn soup. And our great joy when Joseph
and Granny Margaret came through the door.

Granny died when I was in Montreal. I never said goodbye. As I march, I try to build a memory of her rustling
round the house in Canajoharie, her fingers moving; stitch-
ing, sifting, plaiting my sister's hair, her smell of sweet-
grass and smoke. The way she would catch me by the shirt
— or by the ear. I remember her whispery laugh, and how
her shoulders shook with coughing as we walked to
Niagara. She talked all the time of how we'd return to the
Valley. Now she never will.

My mind turns on such thoughts as all the days become
alike. I rise in the dark, snatch a ration of biscuit, set out
again on the trail and march till night. One morning the

sun comes up blood red but soon disappears into a cloud like a blue mountain in the sky. By mid-morning another shower catches us. Wet to bed, wet to go on. My clothes and boots never dry.

So far this raid is slogging in the rain and sleeping in the damp and drinking thin tea over a smoldering fire. We've seen no one and had no battles.

"Soldiering's mostly marching," says Tice.

~ 17 ~
BURNING THE VALLEY

AFTER eight days' steady tramping we reach Cherry Valley. The scouts fan out and we come up through the grain fields and run low through the orchards. But the granaries are empty, and most of the houses and barns lie in ruins.

A few farm folk run ahead of us, hot-footing it through the fields, making for the houses still standing. I hear them shouting, banging the doors closed. Dogs bark, a woman screams, but all else is silent. I take my position behind a tree. I see a small face looking out from an upstairs window, then the shutters clang shut.

If these people seem like ghosts to us, what must we seem to them, as unexpected as if we sprang up out of the earth?

The infantry sets fire to the empty granaries and we march on without a shot being fired. But the Valley knows we're here now, so there's no point in hiding. Speed is what matters. Captain Ross directs us to the main road. It's wider, easier for the horses than the trail, but harder walking. I'm soon ankle-deep in muck. After fifteen miles some are struggling and falling behind.

Sergeant Hayslip roars at the laggards, "If ye can't keep up, there's no one to carry ye. Ye'll be left to the mercy of yer old neighbors. They drove you out once. Don't think they'll welcome ye back more sweetly."

"I'll take my chances," mutters one man. His face is gray-blue, and his ear is bleeding. Another staggers into the bush, doubled over with the runs, dropping his breeches as he goes.

"No one's deserting on my watch," says Sergeant Hayslip, and sends a man after him.

We steal more horses and take sheep and cows where we find them, driving them with us. The cooks will kill them when we stop to eat. They put them in the stew, or give us portions to burn on sticks, Indian style. We don't have time to cook proper, so the meat's tough and black and nearly raw. I find myself thinking of the porridge back at school. A bowl of that wouldn't go amiss now.

I still have the pouch of pounded corn Betsy gave me from Mother. Braves march to war on it, to keep up their strength without needing a fire. Jacob won't touch it, but I take a little when my belly hurts, the way I did when we marched with Mother.

That night the skies clear and a yellow harvest moon rises over the camp. They keep us marching in the moonlight, and near three in the morning we ford Scoharie Creek. "Muzzle the horses and guard yer tongues," Sergeant Hayslip warns us as we empty our boots on the bank. We're within gunshot of Fort Hunter.

We march past a row of charred palisades rising in the moonlight around a square stone building. I know it — Queen Anne's chapel! This must be the Lower Castle, where I went to school and Reverend Stuart preached on Sundays. But the houses are gone and I can't recognize anything else in the night. Not a soul's around. I look back over my shoulder and shudder at the dismal sight.

Suddenly the Seneca next to me peels off and jumps down the gully to the right. He moves so swift that I blink, trying to see where he's gone. The lieutenant notices too and stops the column. "Ready arms."

Two of the Rangers jump into the bush, and the rest of us scouts leave the road, crouching down in the brush.

It's over quick. The Rangers come back leading two rebel militia. One's cut on the head, the blood running down black in the moonlight. Tomahawked, but the Ranger got to him before he was full scalped. The Seneca comes back too, looking fed up.

"Just two of 'em," says the Ranger to Captain Tice, who's come back to see what's going on. My nerves are tingling. I scan the trees, looking for movement, listening hard.

Tice signals the column forward and sends scouts and Rangers off ahead. As we run, I see them leading the prisoners up to Ross and Butler. We travel in silence for another mile before word comes to halt. Everyone leaves the road and takes shelter under the trees. And we wait.

The news they pry out of the prisoners is not good. There's four hundred troops at Schenectady, but not under Willett. He's not off to the east, like we were told. He's back west of Canajoharie, right above us. With four hundred more. And there's five hundred troops beneath us at Scoharie, so we can't go south.

"We're stuck in a triangle, outnumbered at every corner," says Tice. So we'll not be burning Canajoharie. They'd get wind of it straight off and swarm out from the other garrisons.

We wheel about — they don't tell us where to. I only know we're marching away from Canajoharie. I'm glad we won't be burning it. But my hopes of getting to Gitty Hawn's for Peter's violin are fading.

In four hours we halt in the darkness. "Rest on your arms," says Sergeant Hayslip. I drop on the ground, musket between my legs. I can fall asleep in a minute now, turning myself back to front to stay warm without waking.

Two hours later the sky lightens. We're at the edge of a settlement. I don't know what it is until they tell us we're at Warrensbush. That's where Father came to from Ireland, the old village on Uncle Peter Warren's land. We're dead in the middle of Willett's triangle.

"It's the last place they'll look for us," says Captain Butler. "Let's make them remember we were here."

He gives us our orders. The 84th is to provide cover and the 8th to march on. Rangers and Indians to destroy the settlement, seven miles long. That's me — Ranger, scout and Indian all.

"Every granary and haystack, every corn crib, every mill put to the torch," yells Tice, taking over. "Burn the breadbasket, boys, and do it right quick."

Each of us is issued a stout ironwood stick wrapped in

oil-soaked cloth. Jacob and I light our torches and set off to the first barn. For what's left of the night, we burn the whole settlement — not just the granaries and the barns but anything dry enough to catch.

Open the door, torch the hay, fire up the corn crib. We rip cedar shingles from roofs to feed the flames inside. We flush out the stock when we find it and round it up. We mostly stay away from the houses and draw only light musket fire from those with gun slits. It's easily returned by our troops.

The burning barns light the sky, an orange chain in the dark. When dawn comes, the sky's so thick with smoke there's only a dim red glow to show where the sun is. Jacob looks like a scarecrow, face blackened, his lips white where he's licked them. I must look the same.

We meet up with Francis, his uniform sooty and his ginger eyebrows singed. But he's whistling as he goes back for a fresh torch.

"First time I've been dry to the skin since we left the island," he says. "If hell's like this, I won't mind it much."

•••

We're just twelve miles from Schenectady by mid-morning and every building in sight is on fire. The 8th has burnt three mills and a large magazine. Ross, Tice and Butler ride to the head of our advance party and call us to a halt. We fall in, an army of blackened men.

"You've done what we came to do." Ross sounds mighty pleased with us. "There's not a peck of grain left." Though we're exhausted and light-headed from lack of sleep and food, we can still raise a cheer.

"All that's left to do is get out alive before they sniff our smoke. Right wheel up the Mohawk, and we can give Willett the slip!"

They've put us on quick march, and we're moving at a fast clip. But nine days of steady marching is starting to hit the ranks. Rangers don't complain, but some others mutter about food and rest.

"Ain't we going to eat any of those chickens?"

"Time enough when we've put a few miles behind us," says Hayslip. "It'll be your last meal if the Oneidas catch up. They'll have ye roast for dinner, with the chicken inside."

The sun is still lost in blue smoke, but the rain has stopped. Captain Ross says we'll ford the Mohawk at Johnstown. But when we reach it, the river's swollen and rushing from rain. The scouts find the shallowest spot to cross, and the officers order us all to wade into the current.

"Damn me, just when I was dry," sighs Jacob, but he plunges in, calling me to stay close. We're up to my chest at the deepest part, and I have to hold my rifle and powder above my head. A soldier beside me loses his footing. He dips out of sight beneath the rushing water. I grab his coat with one hand just before the river takes him and manage to keep him up, with my other hand holding my musket above my head. Jacob gets his free arm round my shoulder, and we try to steady our footing.

Sergeant Hayslip bellows, "Keep yer wits, or the gulls will peck out yer eyes downstream!" Jacob and I brace the poor fellow between us and we wade forward.

We're almost across and slogging through the silt when

I look up and see a big stone house around the bend. The other two go on but I stop and gape.

I know it. Fort Johnson.

As we walk out of the river and along the road, shots ring out. I watch, amazed. Smoke eddies from a narrow slit in the blocked-up upstairs window — once the sleeping-room I shared with my sisters.

The front door flies open, and out sallies a party of five or six rebels, all shouting and firing. At their head is a big, red-faced man with a pistol in one hand, rum flask in the other.

Major Ross orders a company to form ranks and return fire. With the first volley the rebel officer throws up his hands, and his pistol and flask fly out of them. He stands stock still for a moment, then falls face down in the mud. His leg kicks once and then no more. The men behind him yell in dismay and rush back inside.

"Poor drunk fool," says Hayslip. "He should have stayed in bed."

We don't storm the house. It's crops we've come for, not lives. We've no wish to risk our own. Ross orders us to give the house a wide berth, and we head north up the main road to Johnstown.

"Pick up the pace!" he shouts. I'm cold and wet and dizzy from no sleep. The marching boots and the horses' hoofs ring in my head. And other sounds — the musket fire and the yelling, the thud of the big man falling in the mud.

•••

"Suicide by rum," says Jacob, who can't stay quiet. "How could he hope to come out alive, him and his lot against five hundred?"

But we're not five hundred any longer. We've lost some even in the last two days, through sickness and laggardly marching. More are falling by the wayside. What will happen to them, the ones who've left? The rebels will hang you for deserting. And it's a long way to make it back north on your own, without scouts or Rangers to guide you. Valley folk have shuttered their windows and bolted their doors. Who would take them in, seeing we've burned all their crops? More likely they'll hang them. Or give them to the Oneida.

"How far to Johnstown, Johnson?" Jacob asks. I don't recall. I think when our family moved from Johnson Hall, it took much of a day to get to the river. And we were warm and well fed and riding, not walking and starving in the rain.

We reach the village by mid-afternoon. A few houses are burnt, but most still stand. Captain Tice dismounts, tying his horse to a rail.

"Here's me old tavern," he says, winking at us. "Wait here while I nip in for a snort."

He pushes open the door with the barrel of his gun, pauses for a breath, and goes in. Soon he's back out, shaking his head and frowning. "The buggers haven't left us a drop. But don't put it to the torch, boys. I plan to be back behind the bar by spring."

Ross praises us again on all we've done with so little blood spilled. We're to go in the church to rest a few hours before the push home. The stone walls are strong, and Father built it so big most all of us can fit inside. Some are already stretched out asleep, and two have even curled up by Reverend Stuart's pulpit.

But I can't settle. The crowding brings back the crush of Father's funeral. I know he's right beneath my feet, sealed up in his lead coffin. Peg's not here to pinch me and tell me there's nothing to fear. The air's used up. I turn and fight my way back up the aisle.

"Yer goin' the wrong way, dunderhead!" mutters someone whose boots I step on. Men curse and elbow me, but I'm outside at last.

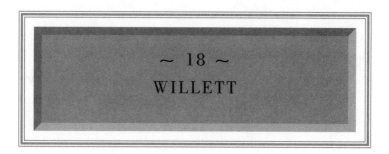

I FEEL better in the air.

"Ho, Johnson!" It's Francis and Jacob, carrying sacks.

"Ross is sending us out to forage," says Francis. "We came to get you. Tell us where to look for food."

Why ask me? After seven years, nothing outside the church seems familiar.

Francis sets off with his musket trained on the shuttered windows. We know there's folks behind them, but we go into their yards anyway. We snatch up hens and ducks and wring their necks and stuff them in our sacks. The garden corn has already been taken in and hidden. The only crops in the ground are rutabagas. I chop some out with my tomahawk.

We make our way through the streets to the end of the village. Up on the hill, through the trees, I see a great white building, five windows across.

"Ho, that's where we came on fair days!" says Jacob. "Once I grabbed a greased pig and had hold of the tail before it skinned away."

"Is that the big house you used to draw at school?" asks Francis, figuring it out. I nod. Johnson Hall, my rightful home — or once it was.

"Might as well have a look then. See what you'll be coming back to."

We limp sore-footed up the broad drive under the bare elms, dragging our sacks. We're careful after the drunken surprise at Fort Johnson, but the house looks empty enough. The front door and most windows are boarded up. The whitewash is peeling from the planks.

I walk around the back to the first stone blockhouse, my musket leveled at the door. This was Father's office. The door's swinging open, hanging on its hinge. I go in and kick at the leaves blown in heaps in the corners and look around. But it's all empty — no desk or tables, no gentlemen. I picture Father's broad back bent over his papers, Mr. Croghan yarning, his gouty foot on a chair.

I look out and see the fields behind are fallow and abandoned. Once they were Mother's gardens, acres of beans and squash and corn. Once there were ponds and fountains and rose walks. Now there's only hayfields, shorn to stubble.

"Will we pass Canajoharie on the route back?" I ask Francis.

He shakes his head. "The prisoners say Willett's still around. Ross'll double us straight back to Carleton Island. Too risky to try to return to the boats."

So we won't be going past Gitty's. I could bolt, but that'd be deserting. There goes my last chance of bringing Peter's violin home.

Back at the church everybody's forming ranks. Ross wants as many miles as he can get between us and Willett. There's no time to cook the fowl, or to sleep, or anything else. I've saved a lump of turnip to chew and a handful of hoarded corn. Jacob somehow kept two eggs unbroken in his waistcoat, and he gives me one.

"Eat up quick, boys, and strip your packs," says Sergeant Hayslip. "This is light march orders. Leave your trophies and bits of iron. We got to put our tails behind us and scurry." We lay off everything not essential — wagons, camp gear, kettles and tents. We're allowed one blanket. They start the companies out at quick march.

We've hardly gone a mile when a scout runs up from the back. "Willett's coming! He's almost at the rear column!"

Fear runs though me like lightning, setting my hair on end. It's here.

Ross wheels us round and we form positions to fight. The rear company's now the front, but our four-pound gun is behind us. The artillery turn it to protect our flank. Hayslip yells at all the scouts to find cover.

I crouch low behind a rocky outcrop, my gun as steady as I can hold it. Minutes ago I was trudging, near the end of my strength. Now I'm so sharp my fingertips tingle. I hear branches breaking and tramping feet and men grunting.

Through my screen of ferns I see something moving. A blue coat! At that instant there's an order to fire. A thunderous roar — smoke rises, a black hat flies into the air and an enemy soldier screams and falls.

"Fire at will!" Tice shouts at us. I steady my musket and

aim into the rebel ranks. Without looking to see if the shot found a mark, I prime the pan, pour in the powder, ram a new charge home.

The infantry's firing by volleys. The noise is deafening. Burning powder stings my eyes and nostrils. A man beside me yelps as an enemy's shot whistles past. He puts his hand to his head and pulls away a bloody hank of hair. He catches my eye.

"Hardly grazed me," he grins.

Prime, pour, ram. The enemy troops fall back. The officers bellow Ross's commands and fire three more volleys, and then call the charge. Rangers and Indians fill the woods with bloodcurdling yells. I'm screaming and running, keeping low, skidding on the rough ground, ducking under branches. We stop to fire at the rebels running before us, reload and run again.

We're fierce and fast and we chase them all back out of the woods. There they are, running in the open! We raise a roar and fire after them. The front of our line takes quite a few down, as the Indians catch up and tomahawk the slowest. The stragglers throw up their hands in surrender, trying to save themselves from Seneca knives.

We're standing and panting for breath when the rebels come at us again. Both our companies strike the same as before, and the coward blue-coats go running. Our warriors race after, tomahawks high, shrieking like nightmare demons.

"Damn me," I hear Tice swear, "if we had more Indians like these we could drive the whole lot back to Albany!"

Tice swings us around to attack Willett's left wing, and

suddenly we're smack in the midst of them. I see a figure raise his weapon above the soldier nearest me and I fire point blank. The rebel pitches backwards, a tomahawk slipping harmlessly from his hand.

I look only once. He's dead, his throat torn away by my shot. His face is red, but not just with blood. War-paint covers the left side of his face. I've shot an Indian in a blue coat.

Blackwater appears beside me. "Oneida. Take the scalp."

I reach for my knife, then back away, shaking my head.

"To you," I say, knowing what will happen. Blackwater flips the man over, plants his knee in the shoulder blades and grabs for the scalplock. As he leans over with his knife, I turn away and reload.

My old gun's getting fouled and the barrel's red hot. It's harder all the time to ram the shot. I've got to choose my targets with care. But I don't know where to aim, where to shoot. I feel and hear the noise all around me — musket shot, screams and yells.

Suddenly a pack of blue-coats are racing straight at me. I fire, someone yells, two men fall. Blackwater is beside me again.

"Two for one," he whoops and rushes on.

A hand grips my shoulder and I nearly jump from my skin. I turn. It's Francis. He pulls me into the cover of a fallen tree where some other soldiers crouch.

"Save your fire," he shouts. "We've got them on the run."

He's wrong. Another line bursts over the ridge, cursing

and firing, without order or command. Francis stands to shout an order, and it's my turn to pull him down as a rebel soldier takes aim at his head.

The shot shatters a branch and spatters bark and leaves in my face. They're almost upon us. I reload and fire and hear an answering scream of pain. A black-bearded shaggy rebel bears down upon us, roaring, his bayonet fixed straight at us. Two men near me fling themselves out of harm's way, but Francis's head is down as he reloads.

My shot is gone. I snatch my tomahawk from my belt and leap forward to bring it down on the man's skull with all my might. Even through the deafening noise I hear the crunch.

Still he hurtles on, but Francis has time to roll aside. The bayonet strikes a rock instead. The man jerks around, blood pouring down his face. He's wearing my tomahawk like an ornament.

His eyes, red as fire, fix on me.

"Devil spawn!" he screams. "Whoreson!"

It cannot be.

Jost Kellock.

He staggers, sags, then crumples. I grab for my tomahawk and try to pull it loose. It sticks, like an ax in a block of wood. I tug on it, hearing Francis shouting at me to leave it, telling me to follow. My tomahawk comes free and I run after him.

We turn our fire on the third division now approaching. In the distance I catch sight of a big man on a horse near the front. He lifts his hat off his yellow hair, pointing toward us.

"That's Willett!" yells Walter Butler, and fires his pistol. Those of us primed and ready let fly with a sharp round.

The woods ring with the blast and dirt, and leaves fly up in the smoke wherever the shot lands. After only a few minutes, the rebels flee the woods yet again. I'm left listening to my heart and the crashing of branches as the last of Willett's troops beats a retreat.

"After them!" cries Walter, and leads a whooping charge back down the hill.

We haven't far to go. Now it's the turn of Willett and his troops to hole up in the Johnstown church. We take cover and watch the doors and windows. I've time to scan our ranks for Jacob. I haven't seen him since the rebels first caught us.

We're filthy with soot and one man looks much like the next. I'm watching for Jacob's skinny form and fair hair.

Where is he?

It's a long time before I find him. His hair is blackened with smoke and his eyes are wide and spooked. One sleeve is torn away. But he raises the arm in greeting, so he's all right. I go to stand by him. He's breathing hard and for once has little to say.

Light rain starts falling and it's turning cold. If we stay here, we'll be caught by their reinforcements. Our losses are counted up and the prisoners readied for the march. Twenty men missing, maybe not all dead. Some ran off in the smoke of the battle, says Francis. Blackwater and his men have their belts hung with scalps, Jost Kellock's among them, no doubt.

Ross leaves a party of scouts behind to keep firing

through the night whenever anyone ventures out the church door. He orders the rest of us once again to start the long road back to Carleton Island. We march six miles into the woods and when it's so dark we can't see, camp for the night. Even if Willett breaks his men out of the church, they can't march in the woods without light.

Before I wrap myself in my blanket I go to the swift-running little stream and strip off my jacket and shirt. In the dimness I see my arms are crusted with blood. I feel it sticky on my face. The cold water stings as I scrub. Some of the blood is my own. But I won't sleep with the blood of Jost Kellock on me.

All night he haunts my dreams.

~ 19 ~
WARRIOR

A T FIRST light we're having a hasty cold breakfast when Walter Butler comes and sits by me. The rest of us are filthy, but somehow he still looks well turned out, like he's going visiting. His face is smooth and scrubbed, and even his scratches are cleaned up.

He sets his hat upon his knee, eyes full on me. "What's your name, lad?"

When I tell him, he says, "I heard you were here. When I'd come up to Johnson Hall, you were a wee lad hanging in the corner. How are your pretty sisters? Still dancing?"

"They're well," I stammer.

"Betsy was one, I mind."

"Betsy's near married," I volunteer, pleased that mighty Walter Butler has singled me out.

"There's the pity." He grins and shakes his head. "She was the likeliest of a likely bunch. Do you remember me, then?"

Suddenly I have a flash of a memory — Johnson Hall on a Fair day, a game of Indian ball, Johnstown against

Butlersbury. All the rest were older, but I scored. The other side's captain growled, "Well kicked, lad." Then he muttered in my ear, "Do it again and I'll break your leg!"

He's smiling at me now. "I cut a fine figure at a dance, if I say so, dancing to Peter Johnson's fiddle. He could play fine, your brother!"

I pluck up my courage. It's the chance I've dreamed of. "You and he fought side by side at St. John's, sir. When Peter took Ethan Allen's surrender."

He looks at me with fresh interest. "Ah, he did. It was your brother was closest to the villain. It could as easy have been me, of course. But it was the making of the boy, and I don't begrudge him it now."

Captain Tice has come up on the other side of the fire. He says something to Walter but Walter doesn't hear. "The devil chooses his partners, eh, lad?" he goes on. "I'm alive and he's dead. And when all's said and done, that's what it comes down to."

"Dead?" I hear myself say the word.

"Just rebel spite, saying it was like a Johnson to die in bed of ague. More likely it was galloping gangrene."

I shake my head. What does he mean?

"He's not dead! We've had letters. Colonel Butler said he wasn't dead. Your own father said so. Wounded, Peter was, in Philadelphia!"

Walter looks at me like I'm simple. "Sure, Peter Johnson took a bullet at Mud Island. And died of it in the end, I hear."

I can't speak.

"Can I have got it wrong?" he finally says. "Have you had word since?"

I nod my head. Letters and letters. Then I look across at Tice. His face tells me what I don't want to know.

A soldier comes and says to Walter that Major Ross wants him. He rises and leaves us. I turn to Tice.

"Is it true? Does she know?"

He looks at me sombrely. "How could she not, George? All those letters was old."

Around me figures are moving, but I've gone somewhere else. Campfire and men are lost. I stand in the middle of a whirling dark.

After a long time I feel a shaking at my shoulder and see Jacob. His lips are moving, talking to me.

"Johnson? Orders is going out to break camp. We got to fall in to get our rations."

I hear screaming.

"They're killing the horses for food."

The provisioners hand out bloody chunks of horsemeat, still steaming. The corn in my stomach rises and I turn away.

Jacob is still at me but I push him off. I go down to the stream by the Indian tents.

Blackwater is sitting by his fire. "I would march with you now," I say to him.

He looks at me for a moment. "You're a white soldier."

"Cut my hair then," I say hoarsely. "I've killed. I'm a warrior."

He looks at me again, saying nothing. At last he reaches for his pouch and takes out his English razor. He motions to me to follow him to the stream. I pull my queue loose and shake my hair around my shoulders. I stand while he lifts a hank and slashes close to my head. A handful falls, and then another, dropping on the ground around my feet. Blackwater works fast, without a word. He frowns in concentration, tongue between his teeth. The blade cuts close, scraping my skull.

Others are shouting at us to make haste, but Blackwater keeps cutting steadily until he has finished. He ties up the long lock he's left and weaves in feathers from his own scalplock.

Then he hands me a small skin bundle from his bag. I unfold it to find red and black paint, wrapped in leaves. I run two black fingers down my cheeks and smear the red in a band over my forehead. It's bear grease and powder. It feels gummy, like blood.

Jacob appears at the top of the rise. "Hi, Johnson, there you are," he cries. "Captain Tice wants you."

He comes closer and his jaw drops. "You look like an Indian!" He laughs uncertainly.

Blackwater laughs too. "Looks like I scalped him, eh?" I feel wetness dripping down my forehead and trickling down my neck. My head stings from a hundred tiny cuts and scrapes, but it's better than the pain inside.

"Tell him I'll come soon."

Jacob shrugs and disappears back up the bank. But I don't follow. I follow Blackwater up the hill. From now on I march with the Indians.

Indians don't chatter. The quiet gives me time to think. One foot ahead of the other, I keep walking. I play my foolish hopes over and over in my head. I hand my chunk of half-raw horsemeat to some Seneca who can't believe his luck. I have no stomach for it.

Three long years. We had letters, yes, but none since Niagara. Peter hasn't been in Philadelphia, dancing at the Whartons' balls. He hasn't been giving the southern rebels a hiding, nor been in England.

He's been dead.

Even my dreams have been nothing but imaginings. I've conjured up a ghost, not a living person. I've been talking to myself all this time.

•••

The trail splits, one path to the north, the other west. I watch the Seneca scouts confer briefly and lead us westward. A few miles on there's angry shouting. Ross has discovered we're leading everyone back to Niagara instead of north to Carleton Island.

He orders us to turn back. The chiefs refuse, and there's more yelling from Ross and Walter Butler. In the end Blackwater and most of the other Indians decide to part company and go west on their own. Tice will go with them and head back to Niagara.

I begin to move down the trail after Blackwater. Someone shouts out my name.

"George! George Johnson, where are you going?" Francis Redding is at my side.

Then Captain Tice is there too, grasping my shoulder roughly. He takes in my shaved skull, and he scowls. "God in heaven! What a bloody scarecrow! Not deserting your company, are you, Johnson? I took your oath myself."

I shuffle my feet, eyes cast down. Slipping out of his grasp, I try to follow Blackwater, who is nearly out of sight.

"George." Tice steps into my path. "George, you must

go back to the island with your company. You swore your oath to the King, and I gave my word to your mother."

We hold each other's gaze. At last I give in with a groan. I turn away from the Indian trail and fall in beside Francis. He grins and tries to shake my hand, but I cannot smile back at him. As we head north, I drag my feet.

Every step is taking me back to a world where they have lied to me. Mother has lied to me. I don't want to return. I don't want to march. Or eat. Or sleep. I don't want anything anymore.

•••

A damp fog fills the valleys as we wearily tramp along. How many days have gone by? One? Two, three? The weather's cold and grim, like my thoughts.

Without warning, a shot cracks the air.

We freeze and look at one another in dismay. Another echo bounces from the cliff in front.

"Damn," cries Hayslip. Scouts come running frantically from the rear.

"Willett!" they shout. "Close on our trail!" He's in pursuit with fresh troops, including a number of Oneida.

Somehow we get across West Canada Creek. While the first company sets off up the trail at a run, Walter Butler gathers a group of marksmen, Francis among them.

"Johnson," Butler calls.

I go, angry but as ordered. I hate the sight of Walter Butler now. He looked at me as if I was half-witted not to know Peter was dead. With luck I'll be killed too. I've painted my face black. That means I'm ready to die in battle.

Butler gives his orders quick. "Line the ford and hold

the enemy until Ross and the others can make a stand. There's better ground a mile or so on."

The stream and woods around are in dense fog. On the other side I make out the first of Willett's men leaning out behind the trees. Butler gives the order and I fire. Before the echo of my shot is stilled, a man falls into the river. My fifth kill? Maybe more. Something to tell Peter, I think, then take the thought back. Let the poor wretch tell Peter himself when they meet in the next world.

I prime and reload. The fog rolls down so thick I can't tell where the enemy are standing. I strain to see their blue coats.

Several more shots are exchanged across the creek, but we can't tell if we're reaching them. The mist is thicker than ever, and Butler takes the advantage to lead us along the bank to a better position.

"We can pick off the whole company if they come across." I scramble up the slope, grasping any branch or root to keep my footing. I try to keep sight of Butler in the white mist.

Now snow is falling too, stinging my face. A sudden wind sweeps down the valley, and for one moment the fog lifts like a curtain. I see clear as anything the men on the other side, their blue coats, their white breeches. And the muzzles of their muskets.

Shots ring out. Musket balls whip past my head and something sears the flesh of my thumb. At that same moment I hear Butler exclaim, indignant.

Then he dives head first into the stream. It's done so smooth I almost laugh — like he's jumped into a swimming hole on a summer's day. But he lands hard in the shallow stream bed, caught by the rocks a little ways away from three fallen rebels.

He doesn't get up. He's limp and still as a rag doll. The stream flows away from him, bubbling red.

The fog closes in again quick as it opened. I start down the cliff, but someone catches my coat tail.

"Where are you going?" It's Francis.

I motion to where Walter fell.

"He's dead, done for," Francis says flatly. "Come on. Let's go."

"He said to hold them."

"They won't follow now. Listen to them."

I hear splashing in the stream. A voice screams out just below, "It's Butler! We got Walter Butler, boys!" They cheer and whoop at the top of their lungs. I hear an Oneida war cry. I know what that means.

I raise my gun to fire, but Francis stays me again. "No, Johnson. Leave them be. That's an order."

We retreat swiftly up the trail. I look back over my shoulder but Francis is right. They have their prize, and no one cares for the rest of us. We hasten to catch the others.

Major Ross watches our approach. I see him look for Walter. "Where is Captain Butler, Corporal Redding?"

"Shot, sir," says Francis. "Killed at once. And scalped, I reckon. Oneidas got him."

Ross closes his eyes.

I hold my breath as the whisperings spread out around us. "Walter Butler! I thought the man had more lives than a bobcat!"

Sergeant Hayslip shakes his head in disbelief. "I said

our losses were light. I spoke too soon." He looks at Major Ross and says what we're all thinking. "Old Butler. Do we send a runner ahead to tell him?"

Ross looks grim. "Time enough, he'll hear. We've got to get the rest of us back with our scalps still under our hats."

We head into a snowstorm. Those as is sick or injured are left behind to make their own way however they can. My hand is still bleeding where the shot grazed my thumb.

They say it's ten days' long march. By the third day our ration of horseflesh is down to half what it was. We're slowing. The weather changes to rain, and those who've lost blankets and greatcoats wrap their arms about themselves, faces wet and grim. We sleep when it's too dark to march and stagger on at first light, all the while listening for sounds of pursuit.

I'm lost in my thoughts, climbing, descending, stopping to bind my blisters, gnawing the raw meat. I think of Peter — and Walter too — in the brave early days of his letters, when each battle was glorious and even the King took notice. What does the King notice now, across the sea in London? Is he feasting and dancing, celebrating the Royal Birthdays, like they read us out in school? Does he even know we're here, stumbling along this mountain trail, fighting this war for him?

The wind comes up, and the whistling sound of it gets in my mind, like the women keening when Father died, or the scream of the peacocks. Sometimes it's like a violin far away in the trees. My hand throbs. Sleet stings my eyes, and my tears make channels through the blood and paint left on my cheeks.

Jacob falls in beside me, all knobs and hollows, his lips cracked open. He's quiet at first, but he's not one to keep still.

"You've hurt your hand," he says. "Best get home and get it tended to, eh? I'm bound to keep body and soul together for Ma and Pa's sake. Got to keep saying that. It keeps your feet moving, eh, Johnson?"

I only grunt in reply, but he goes right on. "Say, do your sisters like sledding? I plan to make a sled when we get back. Go right down the big hill and out on the river. Wouldn't that be fine?" His gabbling takes my mind off the questions going round and round in my head.

Did she know?

Why did she lie to me?

~ 20 ~

HOME

O N THE ninth day at midmorning we break through the trees and come out at the great lake. Carleton Island looms like a dream, silvery under a bruised sky. The snow along the shore isn't deep, so we easily gather piles of driftwood and fire them. Clouds of black smoke billow up. The water between us and the island is calm and we all shout, but it's our signal fires that alert the sentries. Soon a line of canoes is on its way to take us off.

"The whole fort's come down to the wharf to meet you," says the corporal who lands first. We load up wounded and prisoners first, then regimental companies. I go across with the few Indian Rangers who didn't head off to Niagara with Blackwater and Tice.

We've done what we were sent to do and made it back, fifty men short but only a dozen dead for sure, with fifty new prisoners to make up the numbers. But the news about Walter spreads quick, dampening the ragged cheers from the people at the shore.

I pick out Mother and my sisters in the crowd. I don't

know why, but I don't head to them at once. I stand to one side and watch my family bunch together, searching the ranks. The last men alight from the canoes and my mother does not see me among them. Her face is grim.

Now all the canoes are empty, and there are no more to come. Peg is pushing through the crowd to Francis. She's speaking to him. I see him turn and scan the shore. His eyes stop on me. He points.

I go over to them. I've come back with no violin and no one to play it. Ever again.

Mother gasps, taking in my shaved head, the cuts on my face, patches of war-paint. Lana and Betsy huddle behind her, their faces fearful. Mary and Susannah clutch each other's hands. No one makes a move toward me.

"Walter Butler's dead. Oneidas got him. I was there."

Mother doesn't speak, but her lips tighten and her eyes open wide. She reaches up and plucks the bedraggled feathers off my neck.

"What's this? What do you think you're playing at?"

"I was there," I say again. "I spoke to Walter before he died. I asked him about Peter."

This is her chance. I wait, and wait longer, but she makes no answer. She raises her eyes to mine and I see fear in her face.

Suddenly I understand. The truth's sat in her mind all these months, these years, official or not. How could she bear it? And still she hoped. If she doesn't speak about Peter, he's still alive. For her, for all of us.

I reach out and fold my arms around her. She's so small!

I feel her bones under my hands, through her shawl. She's trembling.

I will not make her speak. I know that now.

Peggy rushes up and throws her arms around my neck.

"Georgie," she wails. "Oh, Georgie, we thought you were dead!"

• • •

They've got a hip-bath from somewhere and they fill it with kettle after kettle from the fire while Mother dresses my hand. Then I let them take my filthy rags and sit in the steaming water with my knees up around my ears. Slowly the heat gets through to my bones. Peggy scrubs my head and feels my shaved scalp curiously. Mary and Susannah have a turn, giggling. It tickles.

"You look like Uncle Joseph," says Mary.

"It'll grow out."

"It's growing out already," Peggy says, her head on one side. "We can trim this bit to make it more even."

I shake off her hands. "Not yet."

"I've put out dry clothes for you," Lana says. They've made a new shirt and mended my breeches. "When you're dressed, we've set out a feast."

The table is bright with rush lamps and candles they've saved, and my sisters sit round it. Betsy, smooth and ladylike, Lana, thin and nervy, Peggy with her red hair springing up in the light. Mary and Susannah hug my knees on either side.

Mother sits at the head of the table. "You look like my son again." She smiles.

They all want news. "Did you see Johnson Hall?" Peggy asks. "Have they harmed it?"

I tell them what I remember: the windows boarded over, the gardens flattened. "What about the rose arbors?" they demand. "And the fountain in the pond? Did they smash the shell grotto?"

I didn't see any grotto. I can't tell them what they want to know. They see I've got a different picture in my head and stop their questions and let me eat.

It *is* a feast: baked squash and pigeon pie and honey apples, and a big earthenware jug of beer. It feels good to be among them, and after a while I tell a bit more of the raid. When I get to the man coming out from Fort Johnson, firing his gun, they startle me by laughing. I tell them that we got away from Willett, but that's all I say about that part. No one mentions Walter Butler.

I can't eat much. I'm unused to eating, or sitting. I feel dizzy, as if I'm slipping headlong into a pool of darkness. My clothes feel strange, tight. I go upstairs and take them off and fall into a deep, dreamless sleep.

•••

When I rise again, it's morning. Only Mother is at the table below. The girls have gone out already.

"Let me look at your hand again," she says. She unwraps the bandage and examines it carefully in the light from the window. "It's healing," she says. "Now your feet." She calls Juba to bring a basin of warm water, and they shake their heads at the blackened nails, the oozing flesh of my heels. Mother binds them up with remedies. I thank her and give her a kiss.

"You'll be off your feet for a while. We'll have to find something for you to do."

"I've made my plans," I say, though I've only known it this moment. "I've got to talk to Major Ross."

"I'll go with you."

"I'd go myself, Mother," I say, gentle as I can. "If you please. It's private business."

For a moment she looks to disagree.

"Go then," she finally says. "But nothing in haste, mind."

With my green coat cleaned as best as I can, I head to Major Ross's quarters. In an hour or so his officer tells me to go in.

The Major looks surprised. He hasn't seen me up close with my hair cut.

"You have the look of Captain Brant about you, young Johnson," he says, same as everyone else. "That's as right. You conducted yourself in a way he would be proud. Captain Tice says you're a fine shot and did as well as a man far older. You'll make a good soldier, if your mother can be convinced."

I imagine myself changing my green coat for a bright red one, regimental buttons, two across. I might even win an officer's gorget like Joseph's with George Rex on it. My name, and the King's too, hanging round my neck.

But that's parade details, Sunday turnout. I know this now. Just as I know the business of soldiering isn't coats and buttons and polishing. I look at Major Ross, worn and worried, sitting at his camp desk in his red officer's coat. There's white powder drifted down on his collar, and his gorget needs a shine. His red coat is the badge of King's business. And that's best left in the hands of King's men.

"I've come about my orders, sir." Major Ross puts down his quill and nods.

"With your permission," I say, while my nerve holds, "I keep my mother's accounts. I can write both English and Mohawk, and some French. They say I can cipher as much as I've a mind to. So what I'm asking is, I'd request to stay on in the Department. But not as a scout no more, sir. I'd work here where I'm needed, or when the ice clears, I'd go back to Montreal. I could work for Colonel Claus, if the Governor wishes."

Ross looks at me straight. "You acquitted yourself well, Johnson. As a Ranger and a soldier. There'll be no more raids this winter. I'm sure the Indian Department has work to keep you busy. And I will write to Colonel Claus and the Governor."

●●●

"It's well done," Mother says when I tell her. "Though I am surprised. I believed you wished only to be a warrior."

"So I did once."

"They tell me you were very brave. And you kept your head." She runs her hand over my scalp. "You did not go off with Blackwater and his warriors. They left Ross to make his way back alone."

"They see no sense in fighting the white men's war." ·

"I am ashamed of them."

I wish I could tell her what I know now. Whoever ends this war, rebels or British, the great Council Fire is put out. The tribes are sundered, the villages are gone, our people keep moving west and the settlers take their place. All our fighting won't put our Valley back the way it was. It won't bring back our house, nor Peter's violin. Nor Peter.

"I'll write to Dan Claus," she's saying. "I hear Reverend Stuart is in Montreal, wishing to begin a school. Our people will have great need of learning when the war is finished. There will be many things to settle, when we return. You could be of use."

I scratch my head where my hair's growing in. For a moment I remember the young schoolmaster back in Montreal. Did his scalp itch too, underneath his wig?

There's a sudden commotion at the door. Peg rushes in, pounding the snow from her heels, cheeks flushed. Behind her are Francis and Jacob.

"Come out, come out, George! We've got some bark for sledding down the hill. And, George, there's going to be a ball!"

They decorate the barracks to welcome us back, using up a week's supply of candles. It's warm and bright, away from the snow falling outside.

We're footsore and weary, but we dance. Even I take a turn around the floor with Lana till my feet give out. Then I sit by Mother to watch my sisters whirling amidst the red and green coats. Peggy goes by on Francis's arm, and Jacob jigs up and down despite his blisters.

The fiddlers strike up "The White Cockade." I close my eyes, and in a sudden fancy I see Peter, standing in his red coat, fiddle under his chin. His eyes are closed like mine, and he dips and sways, smiling to himself, his bow flashing. Then a patch of green: Walter Butler whirls by, a girl in his arms, his coat-tails flying.

I squeeze my eyes tight, but the picture's fading. The tune changes to something thin and lilting. Snow is falling all around. Flakes of snow fall thick on Peter, on Walter, on the dancers, sifting across the floor, covering us all.

I open my eyes to a jumble of red and green coats, dipping and gliding. Peter and Walter aren't dancing. They're lying somewhere under a blanket of white, cold and dead. It's us who have to find a way to get on, with the dancing, with the war, with our lives. It's us who have to let them go. Let them rest easy, under the snow.

HISTORICAL NOTE

None of the Johnsons returned to live in the Mohawk Valley. Though no one at Fort Haldimand or Fort Niagara knew it, the British surrendered before George reached the Valley.

For the next few years most of the Six Nations were refugees in their own land, camping outside British forts as they waited for the British, French and Americans to agree on terms.

Joseph and Molly were shocked when, in the Paris Treaty of 1783, there was not one word about His Majesty's Native Allies. It was as if they did not exist. Worse, the British ignored their own treaties, including the Stanwix treaty that Sir William had negotiated. Instead they gave the new American government all the land west to the Mississippi and north to the Great Lakes.

The property of white loyalists was also confiscated, but at least they were able to petition the British government for reparations. Few of the Indians held deeds to private land. Most were now desperately poor, their villages and longhouses burnt, their ancestral lands taken.

Joseph sailed to England a second time in 1785 to petition the King on behalf of the Iroquois Nations. The Mohawk were offered two large tracts of land in Canada. Chief John Deserontyon of Fort Hunter chose land west of Kingston on Lake Ontario and established the Tyendinaga Reserve. Joseph chose 800,000 acres north of Lake Erie on the banks of the Grand River. There he resettled the Mohawks and other families from the Six Nations confederacy, and families of some white soldiers who had fought with him. He built a church, schools and mills, the basis for the modern city of Brantford.

All of Molly's children except Peter survived the war. When

Carleton Island was awarded to the Americans, most families from the garrison moved a few miles north across the St. Lawrence River to Cataraqui. Later renamed Kingston, this city became the first capital of Upper Canada. Molly and Joseph were given land and houses there by the British, which were eventually handed down to Molly's daughters.

Betsy moved to Niagara with Dr. Kerr and had five children. Only Mary remained single, the other sisters marrying military officers. George lived in Kingston but sometime after his mother's death, in 1796, he moved to the Grand River and married a Cayuga woman. In 1825 he was still a schoolteacher at the mission school at Davis's Hamlet near the Mohawk village. Known as Big George, he died a year later and was remembered as a kind and decent man.

TIME LINE

1759: British win the Seven Years' War, defeating the French and securing their hold on North America. Molly Brant and William Johnson's first child, Peter, is born.

1769: Bostonians disguised as Indians throw tea into the harbor to protest taxes.

1773: Boston citizens attack British soldiers and drive out tax collectors.

1774: Quebec Act forbids white settlement on territory belonging to the native peoples. William Johnson dies. First Continental Congress meets in Philadelphia to plan an independent nation.

1775: Skirmish between British troops and colonists in spring in Lexington, Massachusetts. Congress meets again to vote to raise a 20,000-man Continental army led by George Washington. Hundreds of British sympathizers, including Guy Johnson and Daniel Claus, flee their Mohawk Valley homes and head for Montreal, now military headquarters of the British. Ethan Allen and Benedict Arnold capture Fort Ticonderoga and Crown Point on Lake Champlain. Montreal falls after several skirmishes. The Johnsons and Joseph Brant sail to London to petition the King.

1776: British give up Boston and lose Charleston. American independence declared July 4. Joseph Brant and Peter Johnson take part in the British retaking of New York in August.

1777: Washington wins major victories in New Jersey and Vermont. British descend from Canada to fight the local Continental militia at the battle of Oriskany, "the bloodiest battle of the Revolution." Molly Brant and family leave the Valley. Burgoygne surrenders army of 8,000 to rebel forces at Saratoga. Peter Johnson fights at British siege of Philadelphia.

1778: Molly sends George and Peggy to school in Montreal. Joseph Brant raids and burns Cobleskill and Springfield and, with Walter Butler, Cherry Valley. Washington sends Sullivan to destroy native homes and farms all the way to Lake Erie. France joins the war on American side.

1779: Much of the war moves to the south. Molly moves to Carleton Island. Other children start school.

1780: British commander Cornwallis destroys an army in South Carolina, then suffers setbacks. Sir John Johnson leads raids on the Mohawk Valley.

1781: George takes part in final raid on Johnstown under John Ross and Walter Butler. Lord Cornwallis surrenders to the Americans.

1783: Peace treaty negotiated in Paris. All Indian lands in New York given to Americans by the British. British forts on the U.S. side must be vacated, including Fort Haldimand on Carleton Island. Molly and her family move to Cataraqui, present-day Kingston.

HISTORICAL CHARACTERS

This is an imagined story about the following real people. All other characters are fictional, though their names may be taken from historical records.

Abram: House slave at Johnson Hall.

Allen, Ethan: b. 1738. Led Green Mountain Boys on an attempted invasion of Canada. Took Fort Ticonderoga, then was captured by Peter Johnson at Montreal.

Andrews, Captain: Ship captain on the Great Lakes. Went down with the ship *Ontario* in a storm on the lake in 1780.

Arnold, Benedict: b. 1740. American general in Revolutionary War. Took Fort Ticonderoga with Ethan Allen. Later defected to British.

Bloomfield, Captain Joseph: Continental officer, 3rd New Jersey.

Bolton, Colonel Mason: King's 8th Regiment, commander at Fort Niagara.

Boone, Daniel: b. 1735, Pennsylvania. Frontiersman, fought in Revolutionary War in the west.

Brant, Joseph (Thayendanegea): b. 1742, Ohio Valley. Grand chief of the Six Nations. Educated at Wheelock School (later Dartmouth College), secretary to Guy Johnson. Captain in the British forces during the Revolutionary War.

Brant, Margaret Cananaradunka (Granny): Mother of Joseph and Molly.

Brant, Molly (Degonwadonti, Konwatsi'tsiaienni): b. 1736, Ohio Valley. Grew up in Canajoharie as stepdaughter of Terihoga (Chief Sachem) Brant. Consort of Sir William Johnson from 1759 to his death in 1774. Later head of

Iroquois clan mothers and negotiator between British and Indians.

Butler, Walter: b. 1752. Lawyer, officer in King's 8th and captain in Butler's Rangers. Sentenced to hang as a spy, escaped to Canada. Killed on Valley raid.

Butler, John: b. 1728 in Connecticut. Second biggest landholder in Mohawk Valley. Fought with William Johnson at Niagara, Lake George, Fort Frontenac and Montreal. Deputy to Guy Johnson at Niagara, led Butler's Rangers on raids at Oriskany, Mohawk and Wyoming Valleys.

Cato: House slave at Johnson Hall.

Chew, Joseph: Executor of Sir William's will, guardian of the children. Secretary for Indian Affairs in Canada.

Claus, Daniel: b. 1727 in Germany. Joined Indian agent Conrad Weiser on a trip to the Mohawk in 1749. Boarded with Joseph and Molly in Canajoharie, became Sir William's agent in Montreal. Married Anne (Nancy) Johnson. Superintendent of the Canadian Indian Department.

Claus, William (Billy): b. 1765. Grandson of Sir William. Lieutenant, 1st Battalion, King's Royal Regiment of New York, later deputy superintendent for Indian Affairs at Niagara.

Croghan, George: b. 1720 in Ireland. Trader, land speculator, interpreter. Deputy superintendent of Northern Indian Affairs under Sir William. Joined Continental army, died in debt from land speculation. Daughter Catherine married Joseph Brant.

Dease, Dr. John: b. 1745 in Ireland, son of Sir William's sister Anne. Sir William's physician.

de Lisle, Reverend: Swiss-born Anglican preacher, headmaster of George's school in Montreal.

Franklin, Governor William: b. 1730, natural son of Ben

Franklin. Last royal governor of New Jersey. Land speculator with George Croghan and Sir William. Arrested by New
Jersey Congress in 1776, exiled to England.

Fundy, Jane (Jenny): Johnson Hall house slave, younger sister to Juba. Left to Molly in William's will.

Fundy, Juba: Johnson Hall house slave, sister of Jenny.

Haldimand, Sir Frederick: Swiss-born British soldier, served
in French and Indian War at Ticonderoga and Oswego.
Military commander in chief of Canada, governor of Quebec.

Herkimer, Nicolas: Third generation Palatine, brigadier-gen-
eral of Tryon County Militia. Ordered arrest of Sir John
Johnson in 1776 and led forces at Oriskany, where his brother fought on loyalist side. Died following battle.

Hill, David (Karonghyontye): Mohawk chief. Leader on last
Valley raid. Portrait (with Guy Johnson) painted by Benjamin
West.

Johnson, Anne (Nancy): b. 1740. Daughter of Sir William
and Catherine Weissenberg, married Daniel Claus. Two children, Billy and Catherine.

Johnson, Anne (Annie): b. 1773. Youngest child of William
and Molly. Married naval captain Hugh Earl. Three children,
Anne, Mary, Jane.

Johnson, Brant (Kaghneghtago): c.1740. Mohawk son of
William. Married a white captive and served at Niagara with
Butler's Rangers. Daughters educated in Montreal.

Johnson, Elizabeth (Betsy): b. 1761. Second child of
William and Molly. Married Robert Kerr, surgeon. Four children, William, Walter, Robert, Nancy.

Johnson, George: b. 1768. Fifth child of William and Molly.

Johnson, Colonel Guy: c. 1740. Irish-born nephew of Sir
William. Married his cousin Polly Johnson in 1763. Served
in French and Indian War, became superintendent of

Indian Affairs after Sir William's death. Died in England.

Johnson, Sir John: b. 1742, son of Sir William and Catherine Weissenberg. Married Mary Watt of New York. Served in French and Indian War, inherited hereditary baronetcy at age 21. Lieutenant-colonel of King's Royal Regiment of New York. Developed loyalist settlements in Canada. Fourteen children.

Johnson, Magdalene (Lana): b. 1763. Third child of William and Molly. Married John Ferguson, MLA, Kingston.

Johnson, Margaret (Peggy): b. 1765. Fourth child of William and Molly. Married Capt. George Farley, 24th of Foot. Four children, Daniel, Thomas, Mary Ann, Fanny.

Johnson, Mary (Polly): b. 1744. Daughter to William Johnson and Catherine Weissenberg. Married Guy Johnson.

Johnson, Mary: b.1769. Sixth child of William and Molly.

Johnson, Peter Warren: b. 1759. First child of William and Molly.

Johnson, Susannah (Suky): b. 1772. Seventh child of William and Molly. Married Lt. Henry Lemoine. Son Edward died at birth.

Johnson, Sir William (Warraghieyagey): b. 1715. Emigrated from Ireland in 1738 to manage properties for uncle Admiral Peter Warren on Mohawk River. Learned native languages and customs, adopted by the Mohawk. Gained baronetcy for defeating the French at Lake George, Fort Niagara and Montreal. Superintendent of the Northern Department of Indian Affairs for North America. Second-largest landholder in New York. Negotiated Treaty of Fort Stanwix (located at present-day Rome, N.Y.) in an attempt to preserve northern and western Indian lands.

Johnson, William (William of Canajoharie, Tagawirunte): b. 1750. Mohawk son of William, mother unknown. Raised at

Canajoharie. Reported living at Brantford at the end of the war.

Kerr, Dr. Robert: Surgeon with the British army, stationed at Fort Haldimand and Fort Niagara. Married Elizabeth Johnson in 1783.

Kirkland, Reverend Samuel: Missionary to the Oneida. Educated at Wheelock's school, Continental chaplain at Fort Stanwix. Directed many Oneida to the rebel cause at Washington's command.

Ross, Major John: Commander of Fort Haldimand, Carleton Island. Led raid to Mohawk Valley in 1781.

Sayayenguaraghta: Chief sachem of Onondaga.

Schuyler, Philip: Member of old, wealthy New York family. Major-general, head of Northern Department. Planned Quebec campaign but gave command to Montgomery when ill. Became U.S. senator; daughter married Alexander Hamilton.

Senhouane: Seneca chief.

Stuart, Reverend John: b. 1740, Pennsylvania. Anglican missionary to the Mohawk at Fort Hunter. Arrested in Revolution, exchanged to Montreal in 1781, founded English school. Founded St. George's Anglican church in Kingston, chaplain to the Legislature.

Tice, Gilbert: b. 1739, Fort Hunter. Tavern-keeper, ranger, commander of Indians, based at Fort Niagara. Fought Ethan Allen at Montreal, negotiated with Willett at Stanwix, served on Valley raids.

Tilghman, Colonel Tench: b. 1744, Maryland. Aide-de camp to General George Washington. Carried dispatches of Cornwallis's surrender to Congress.

Warren, Admiral Sir Peter: b. 1703. William Johnson's uncle. Married Susannah De Lancey, sister of lieutenant-governor of New York. Took Louisbourg in 1745, awarded large tract of land in Mohawk Valley.

Watt, Mary (Polly): Wife of Sir John Johnson. Mother of fourteen children.

Weissenberg, Catherine (Caty): c. 1739. Palatine immigrant, perhaps indentured servant, mother of William Johnson's white children, Anne, John, Mary.

Willett, Marinus: b. 1730. With Montgomery and Ambercrombie at Ticonderoga, Bradstreet at Fort Frontenac. Lieutenant-colonel of 3rd New York. Captured Walter Butler at Shoemaker's tavern, rebuilt Fort Stanwix, served on Sullivan-Clinton expedition. Mayor of New York, 1807.

Yosts: Palatine settlers, Mohawk Valley.

FURTHER READING

Most of the characters in this book were real people. Finding the facts about their lives, however, can be difficult. William Johnson and Joseph Brant had their pictures painted and left us many letters and documents, and so did Sir John Johnson, Dan Claus and Rev. John Stuart. But we don't have pictures of Molly Brant or any letters we can be sure that she wrote, only a handful of comments from people who knew her. There is one poignant oil painting of Peter, painted after his death from a miniature, which can be seen in the collection of the Toronto Public Library. And we can read Peter's letters from Philadelphia to his family, along with several from Peggy written later on in life. But there are no known paintings of any of the other children.

Despite the lack of documents, many have tried to understand the personal lives of the Johnsons and the Brants. Some earlier books made historical mistakes, even mixing up or inventing family members and passing on legends and stories that weren't true. Two books written in the 1990s, *The Three Faces of Molly Brant* by Earle Thomas and *Molly Brant: A Legacy of Her Own* by Lois Huey and Bonnie Pulis, have done a good job of separating fact from story and giving us a better picture of the family and their times.

Novels written about the Loyalists and the Americans in the Revolutionary War for Independence also tell the stories of those caught up in the war from different viewpoints. Books with a Loyalist background include Janet Lunn's *The Hollow Tree*, Mary Alice Downie's *Honor Bound*, Mary Fryer's *Escape* and Connie Crook's *Flight*. James and Christopher Collier's *My*

Brother Sam Is Dead portrays a family with divided allegiances, as does Scott O'Dell's *Sarah Bishop*. Books with an American focus include Esther Forbes' classic *Johnny Tremain*, set in Boston, Avi's *The Fighting Ground*, about the battle of Trenton, and the Colliers' *War Comes to Willy Freeman*.

Very few books on this period have been written from the viewpoint of native people. *The Second Bend in the River* by Ann Rinaldi tells the story of Tecumseh, the Shawnee chief who fought with the British and Canadians in the War of 1812, when the Americans tried again to conquer Canada, and the sons and grandsons of the Johnsons, Brants and Butlers went to war once more.